To Em and Alistair, Love

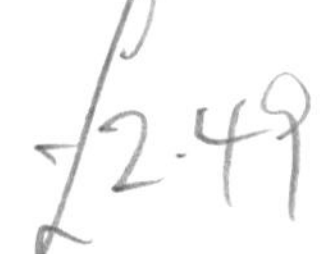

Yo
the Co

Dennis Harkness

With illustrations by Juliet Harkness

"If this were played upon a stage now, I could condemn it as an improbable fiction"

(Twelfth Night II,iv)

To Felix, Hector and Timandra,
and the memory of Joe
My very special children

Translator's Note

In July 1989, Danish archaeologists investigating the ruined foundations of the original Abbey at Roskilde, outside Copenhagen, came upon a long-buried cavity. Within it lay a manuscript. Remarkably well preserved, this document was at first thought to record a previously unknown saga of the Viking era. Then Professor Jan Mjolbjy, Director of the National Museum, examined it. She was astounded to realise that the manuscript comprised an autobiography of one of the most enigmatic figures in Danish history.

It has been my privilege to translate Yorick's Confessions and thus to bring to the English-speaking world the extraordinary truth about the court jester who, as the document makes clear, features in no less than ten of Shakespeare's dramas.

Light is cast too on another little known courtier of those far-off times when Denmark was free of the Norwegian yoke. I refer to Osric. He was clearly a talented playwright. It is indeed quite possible that our own immortal Bard of Avon was inspired to pen his 'Hamlet' after seeing a performance of Osric's play by some travelling troupe.

CAUTION: the translation of Osric's drama is of course my own copyright. Any public performance of the same may take place only with my permission.

Dennis Harkness,

Redwood, TA5 1JE, Somerset, United Kingdom

Chapter One

Roskilde

"Last scene of all,
That ends this strange eventful history"
[As You Like It, II,vii]

This might sound callous but I'm pleased about the Abbot's disability. He is stone deaf. Of course, it's sad that he can no longer enjoy the thrush's glorious morning melody; or the plainsong of the Brothers. But there's another symptom of his ageing. Total obstinacy! He insists on being my personal confessor. And as he cannot hear my words, he demands that I record them on vellum (costly, although the coffers of Roskilde's Abbey can afford it). What's more he wants the whole

of my long history. Presumably he fears that as I approach my own dotage I am in danger of departing this life unpurged of some half-forgotten sin committed during the lives I led before retirement here. Or perhaps he simply enjoys a good yarn.
The task gives me a deep satisfaction. For I am hereby licensed to spend long hours revisiting my years of tragedy and joy, despair and triumph. And in the process I constantly bless the name of Father Gregory, the Court Chaplain at Elsinore during my youth. It was he who first encouraged me to keep a personal journal. This I have maintained, intermittently, with, I hope, sufficient detail to feed this, the story of my life.

People believe me long dead. A garrulous gravedigger once reeled out the first entertaining tale that came into his head and Hamlet believed it. So did the whole world, after the same sexton unearthed the skull of some taverner killed in a brawl – and designated it mine. The myth was made flesh. Or bone, rather. 'I knew him, Horatio,' averred the sweet prince. Ha! Forty years ago

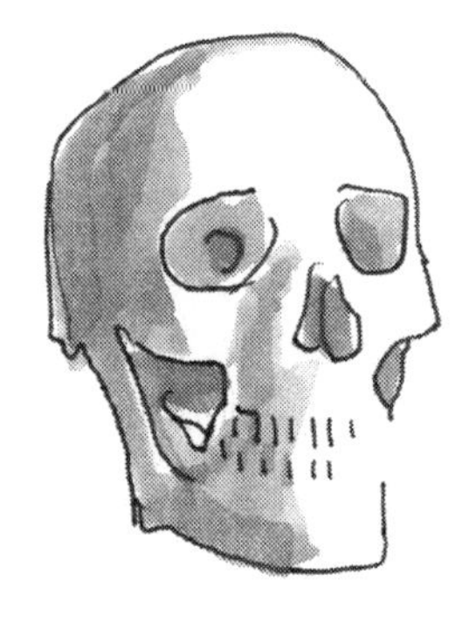

he knew me. Wouldn't recognise me now! Or realise that I am —. But I mustn't get ahead of myself.

Please do not conclude that I am bitter. Far from it. This present peace of mind stems from my having survived past errors and then been granted the chance to atone. In my life I have saved the lives of both my own child and my one true love. Not to mention having restored to Denmark its rightful monarch.

Chapter Two

The Decision

"... flashes of merriment, that were wont
to set the table on a roar..."
[Hamlet V,i]

What need I tell you about my first twenty-five years?

My beautiful black-haired mother died when I was ten. She worked in the court at Elsinore. My father was a sea captain who disappeared on a voyage to Cadiz before I was born. Or so I was told. Later in life my knowledge of the ways of the world led me to doubt the existence of this elusive mariner. Take note of this – the left ear of the old king's youngest brother was deckled. It uncurled at the top. And so does mine. Ahem! A fanciful idea, you think? For what reason then was I, as an orphan, taken under the wing of the Royal Family and granted an occupation and an education?

I benefited from two very different tutors. Father

Gregory, Chaplain to the Court, was my schoolmaster. At the same time I was apprenticed to Crispin, the English jester. Both commented on how quick a learner I was. By the age of fifteen I could write and converse in Danish, Latin, English and Italian (Fr Gregory had studied at Assisi under the Blessed Francis). I had also picked up the basics of his skills as an apothecary. Meanwhile I was understudy to Crispin as Elsinore's favourite entertainer, thanks to the generosity of his tutelage. But I was struggling with a dilemma. My vocation. An extract from the journal of my fifteenth year:

This morning early I knelt in the chapel, desperate for guidance. Last week, Father Gregory advised that I should follow my calling to join the brotherhood of the Franciscan Friars. Yesterday, Crispin's reaction to this proposal was to grab his slapstick and beat me about the ears.

"Ouch! Why?" I demanded.

"Why? You ask me why?" he said in his comical English accent, "I shall tell you why. Because, Yorick, my little idiot-child, God's ambition for you is blazingly obvious. You were born to entertain the faithful, not to waste your time saying prayers for them. You a friar? Pah! Can you imagine never again being permitted to make people laugh? Those eyebrows of yours; that ungovernable haystack of ginger hair; your mighty thighs! All created for a tumbling, bumbling clown, not some sanctimonious saint locked away in a hermit's cell! To say nothing of your skill as a bandolinist."

He was unstoppable. "No more of this nonsense! You'll be the Court Jester in Elsinore long after I am buried. Your name will be famous for it." He paused to think for a moment, then went on, "And if you don't believe me, ask your patroness, the Princess Karin. She won't beat about the bush."

This advice I accepted. In the five years I'd been a ward of court, the King's sister had always taken a special interest in my welfare. So, after supper last evening I waited until she had retired. After a short time, I mounted the spiral steps and tapped on her door. It was opened by the maid. Glancing past her, I could see that the Princess had already begun to undress. I averted my eyes but not before registering how youthful she looked. Rumour had it that she was almost forty but I could not have believed that. Long fair hair lay loose about her bare shoulders. Turning her face to the doorway she smiled, signalling for me to enter. She whispered something to the maid, who laid more logs on the fire and then withdrew.

I surveyed the room while the Princess collected something from the anteroom. The bedchamber was warm. Heavy drapes around the bed were open, with eiderdowns and furs turned back ready to receive her. A lamp glowed on the table alongside.

The odour of burning oil, mingling with smoke from the applewood in the hearth, created a cosiness in the chamber, despite its size.

As she returned, she took my hand and kissed me on the cheek. Her perfume was rich and tantalising. She walked me hand in hand to the cushioned window-seat and sat close beside me. After an awkward moment, I said, "I've come to ask your advice." She answered with an encouraging smile. I launched into explaining my dilemma. Friar or funster, which path should I pursue?

Her response took me by surprise. Still holding mine, she placed her other hand gently on my cheek and turned my face to hers. She kissed me on the mouth. I gripped the cushioned seat, taut with embarrassment. Her tongue tickled my lips. Her hand sidled about my neck, holding my face to hers in a closeness I felt little inclined to bring to an end. But suddenly it did end. To my disappointment, she let go of me. She strode to the door. "We don't want to be disturbed," she said. Her voice was husky. She slid into place the solid wooden bolt. "But we do need warming up."

From an alcove she produced a narrow-necked stoneware jar. Removing the stopper, she filled two goblets which she brought to the windowseat. "Try this," she said. The liquor's fume alone made me dizzy as I watched her take a long quaff. She grunted in approval. "Go on!" she insisted. I took a few sips then a deeper draught. It was some kind of spirit which scalded its way down my gullet. I choked a little then laughed.

"What is this stuff? Lava from the burning mountains of Iceland?"

"From Iceland, yes, but not lava. They call it brennevin – 'Black Death' to the locals, when they take too much of it."

The heat of the drink suffused my senses. "Not a bad way

to go!" I said, thinking at the time that my quip lacked the wit or originality she'd have expected from a Court Jester.

Her eyes were fixed on mine. "I can think of a better way," she purred as she put down her goblet and relieved me of mine. She took my hand again and led me to the bed. We sat on its edge and kissed. This time, emboldened by the drink and her example, I began to give as well as to receive pleasure, a trade which I was excited to realise drew from her the most seductive sighs. When she leapt to her feet therefore I was somewhat put out. But not for long.

"Off with your clothes and into the bed!" she ordered, and as I hesitated, "It's a royal command."

She disappeared into the anteroom. When she returned she was naked. So too, under the bedcovers, was I. She climbed in beside me. Her scented body, pressed softly against the length of mine, quickly stimulated a condition which hitherto only my own imagination had ever achieved.

"You're a big boy," she whispered. I glowed with priapic pride. "How old did you say you were?"

"Fifteen," I gulped as I felt which part of me she was now caressing, "Well, nearly."

"Mmmm!" she replied. At least I think it was a reply.

So next morning there I was, knelt in the Chapel Royal. In my head, prayers for guidance jostled with the afterglow of the night just gone. Lord God, I hear you calling me. But whither? Jesus Christ forgive me that even now my cock is standing on end at the memory of her body, her abandon, my explosions within her.

Someone lifted the latch of the chapel door. I tried to concentrate on the image of Christ crucified, but failed. Perhaps it was the Princess at the door! Between my fingers

I saw instead Crispin, dressed in his red and yellow quarters. Bells jingled as he beckoned me to him. Reluctantly, I rose from my knees and joined him in the courtyard.

"Well?" he asked.

"Well what?"

"Has it helped you to decide? Did our hospitable princess manage to convey what you'd be missing?"

"Missing?"

"If you take your vows of chastity and so on! Are you ready to abjure the intimacy of women, now that you've had a taste of what's on offer?"

"How did you know?"

"Let's say that I have an understanding with a certain unmarried lady of high birth who knows how to enjoy herself. And when yesterday I happened to mention that a budding young stallion of my acquaintance was considering voluntary castration, she and I agreed what a shame that would be." I stood there speechless. He added, "Aren't you grateful?"

"To her, yes! To you, I'm not so sure. Is this how you go about matters in England?"

"That would be telling, my little jester-in-waiting. Talking of which, I need you this evening for the Queen's birthday banquet. Come early. We need to set up for the jousting routine."

The Jesters' Joust! My favourite act of all, when Crispin and I charge at each other up and down the aisles, mounted on hobby horses whose frames hang from shoulder straps. "I'll be there!" I called after him.

Stopping in his tracks, he turned and came up close. "By the way," he whispered in my ear, "The fair princess is looking forward to seeing you again tonight. I believe you've made quite a hit." With that, he made a suggestive gesture with his slapstick and swaggered off in the direction of the kitchens, where he would no doubt wangle a hearty breakfast from the duty cook.

Left at the chapel door, I decided not to resume my devotions. The die was cast. But how am I to explain to the good Father Gregory that my true vocation is not to the monastic life but to the merry?

So far, so obedient to the divine Will! And so it goes for another ten years. I am infinitely witty, or so my reputation says. I become the Court Jester and fulfil my destiny. Until *SHE* smiles at me and robs me of my heart.

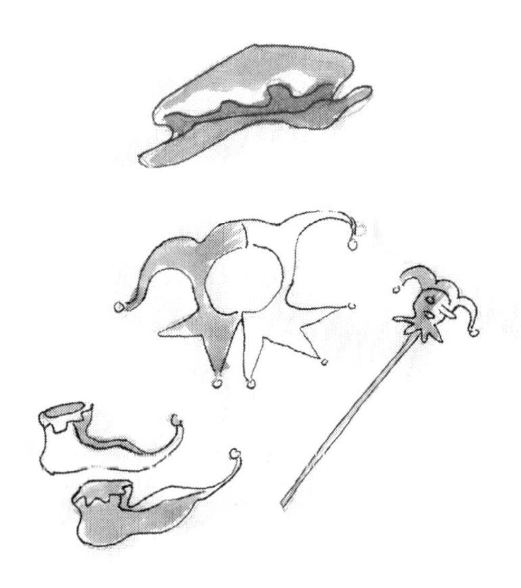

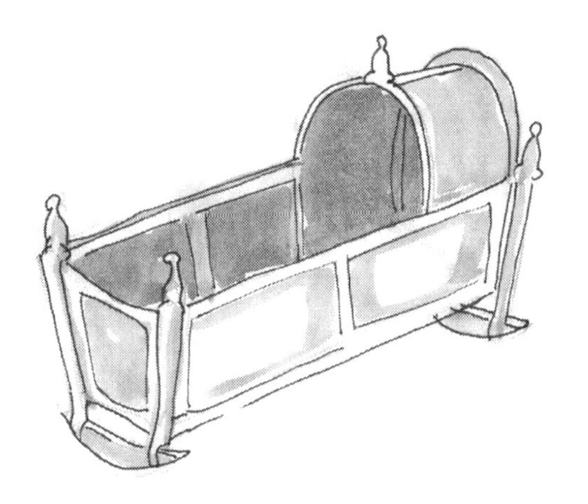

Chapter Three

Birth and Blossoming

"The Child is Father of the Man."
[Wordsworth, 'My heart leaps up']

But back to my beginning. In a nutshell it is this. You may be forgiven for doubting my very first memory. But even after seventy long years I am able to revisit it.

It comes at some moment during the slow metamorphosis from embryo to foetus. Quite gradually I become aware of a steady rhythm throbbing all around, echoed by a quicker lighter beat from within me. From time to time I experience the ambiance of a tender voice, a voice I already love. Its music pleasures my entire being.

I am cushioned all about so that whenever I flex a limb the softness yields a little. Sometimes when a mild spasm makes me kick out, the dear voice chuckles and I feel a response as if a larger limb is pressed against the sachet that surrounds me. I am safe here, beloved, nourished, deeply content.

Such luxury cannot last. I wake from a sleep sensing anxiety in the blood. I hear the adored voice sounding shrill. Its squeal tells of pain; I share this discomfort as pressure builds about me. My fluid cushioning leaks away. There are other voices, gentle, encouraging, but I am helpless. I'm squeezed. Then allowed to relax. Not for long. A more hideous pressure! Ah, let it be. A resignation, a numbness overcomes me. Until …

Inundations violate me. Pain, as cold air floods my lungs. Light attacks my eyes. My ears are invaded too, with unmuffled noise. My skin stings as it is washed and wiped and briskly wrapped. Lost, I peer into the mist. Firm hands enclose me, lift me, lower me. For the first time I breathe in that odour which means I am safe. The beloved voice speaks. The scent too is hers. With infinite tenderness she touches my face and I squint upwards to seek the shape of hers. At my mouth a sweet-smelling mound exudes the invitation to suck. My mother's first gift. I accept it. A new enjoyment. As I surrender to sleep I hear her first words to me. "My darling little Yorick," she whispers.

Thus my earliest memory derives from contentment succeeding trauma. My next springs from joy.

I am seven years old, all eyes are on me and the royal court is rocking. In the Great Hall at Elsinore every person, even His Majesty the King, is laughing. And all because of me! I am hysterical with happiness. My heart is bursting with an ecstacy of suppressed giggles.

I hide it. Resisting hysteria I strut across the torchlit

hall in imitation of the pompous Norwegian ambassador. I glare up into the face of our nation's young First Minister, the Lord Polonius, who collapses slapping his thighs. Tears of mirth in his eyes, he fumbles for the leather purse at his belt, extracts a coin and hands it down to me. It is a weighty one. I make a show of sniffing it, peering at it in scorn. I pretend to test its authenticity between my teeth (or rather the gums where my mother assured me my second teeth would soon grow). Still mimicking the Norseman, I scowl at Polonius, this time sticking out my tongue. Imagine! Making faces at the new Prime Minister! There is no limit to my licensed impudence and the grown-ups love it.

Over the hubbub the King calls out for me to attend him. I note the craning necks of those on the far side of the banqueting tables. Why should I deny *them* a view of my antics? The King, impatient, beckons for me to approach. He is accustomed to obedience, especially from us of low birth.

With blithe impertinence I turn my back on him. I scamper to my mother in the dark corner by the kitchen entrance where she has been watching. I hand her the coin. She gives me a quick hug before pushing me towards the King. Bouncing back into the torchlight I fling myself towards the opposite end of his long table. I hazard a cartwheel, my first in public after plenty of secret practicing. It works! A round of applause! With a hop and a reckless skip I vault successfully (bliss!) onto first a bench and then the refectory table itself. Here I repeat my impersonation of the Norwegian, squinting down my nose at the hot-cheeked diners on either side. Stepping heedless on platters of unfinished meat. Upsetting beakers so that the drink spills and drips on revellers' laps. There are no protests. This is a victory celebration. We the brave Danes have defeated the Norse army of old Fortinbras and I can do no wrong.

Dancing along the table, I reach His Majesty. I stand upright above him. I bow to him in mock solemnity, at the same time lifting the back of my tunic so that the assembled company gets a good look at my bare bum. There are whoops and guffaws. Stroking his grey beard the King rises to his feet. He is no longer smiling. Silence descends, but I know that his anger is a pretence. Bowing to him again, I push out a high-pitched fart, then spin round as if to catch the culprit. Behind me I hear the King's snort of merriment. Such joy! I snatch up the nearest beaker. It is the King's brother's, and half full. I drain it. The richness of the liquor is new to me. It heats my throat with its sweetness. It tickles and catches in my gullet.

I decide to act drunk. Still high on the heavy oak board, I mimic the staggers and belches of the celebrating soldiers I observed all afternoon in the streets below the castle. I lurch helpless towards His Majesty. Find myself falling. He notices and holds out strong arms to catch me.

"Time for bed, my little clown!" he murmurs in my ear. I am dizzy. At his signal a servant glides forward to receive me and carry me to my mother. She kisses me and snuggles me to her perfumed shoulder. She is beautiful, my mother. All men love her, I know. She loves me. I love her. I wrap my arms about her neck and stroke her soft skin. I am sleepy.

Chapter Four

Orphaned

"I am sick at heart"
[Hamlet, I,i]

How, later, did I become a ward of the royal court? Another all too vivid recollection tells the tale.

I am searching for my mother. I am desolate without her. When today, my tenth birthday, they brought me back from the island, I told my guardian, the King's younger sister Princess Karin, how excited I was at the prospect of seeing my mother again. She nodded and looked away as if something on the quayside had caught her attention.

The gesture reminded me of her mood when we embarked with all the palace staff and ministers, a long half-year before. I had demanded to know why my mother was not coming with us. Because, said the Princess, there was no room on board. Not true, I pointed out. She could easily fit among the stores stowed in the longboat's well. The voyage to Laeso was short, I said, less than a day. No, she explained, the space was needed for extra oarsmen who would join us later. But they never did. Besides, she went on, my mother was still poorly. She could follow on with a later party.

It was true that my mother was unwell at the time. I had heard her groans through the pine log wall which divided our little house into two chambers. Once or twice she had let out a cry of pain, which frightened me; but not as much as when I peeped through the elk hide drape that served as a door. She was thin, wasted, lying there in the dim light of a smoky tallow candle; so unlike her glowing bonniness of only one week before. I longed to go to her, to give her one of my special hugs that she loved so much, but my aunt caught me by the shoulder and hustled me into the street. I hated it out there, among the wailing women who, daily it seemed in those days, trod mournful processions following the coffins down the hill to the graveyard.

At first I hated it too on the sandy island of Laeso. Not one of my playmates from the town was there. Apart from the Prince Hamlet, himself scarcely eight, and his baby brother Claudius, I was the only child in the retinue. However, as the weeks went by I began to revel in the attention I received from the King and Queen. They would ask me to perform somersaults and cartwheels, to mimic characters from Elsinore and to sing songs I had learnt from the Italian troubadour who had stayed at court the previous year. Best of all, they allowed me to act as cheeky pageboy to English Crispin, whenever his foolery was called on to lighten the glum atmosphere in the windswept encampment.

Months later, as soon as the boat touches the jetty at

Elsinore I leap ashore. I run at top speed up the hill to our house. At the door a stranger greets me. My mother is not there. I demand to know where she is, but the grizzled fellow can tell me nothing.

"Same as the rest of 'em, I dare say," he wheezes.

"The rest of who?"

"The rest o' they poor souls, God have mercy on 'em, as were took by the pestilence. I'll wager you'll find her in the graveyard, lad."

He is lying, I know it. I spin on my heel and leave him gawping. He is lying, but I run down to the cemetery anyway. I used to play here when I was little; hide and seek among the pillars of stone that marked the graves of the big-wigs, the merchants and chiefs of the court. Now it looks different. The walled enclosure is a morass of turned earth. The adjoining paddock too is pocked with recently dug mounds.

Behind a bank I hear laughter. I recognize the voices of the labourers who come into town when someone has died. They dig the graves and fill them in when the mourners have left. These men are always full of dark fun and know lots of jokey songs, some of which they taught me. I sing these ditties to amuse my friends. My mother loves it when I come up with a new ballad. I am always aware of her pride when I perform for other people, especially at the Court. And I feel proud of her too. She is so beautiful and warm. No wonder the King's brother has an eye for her and wants her to serve at royal banquets. He even visits her sometimes in the winter when the nights are dark and long.

Perhaps she is already at the castle, helping to prepare for the return of the King and the little Princes. I hurry up the narrow streets. The royal party is even now reaching the drawbridge. Folks line the route to cheer them, but fitfully, not with the full-blooded roars which welcomed the King's return from victory over Norway.

I catch up with the procession and slip in alongside the Princess Karin, who squeezes my hand. She keeps hold of it and takes me with her up the stone steps to her chamber, high in the palace's eastern tower. I have never been here before. Rich fabrics deck the plastered walls and a high-curtained bed fills one side. The chambermaid busies herself in an anteroom as Karin draws me to sit alongside her in the windowseat. She sighs. We remain in silence for a while. I wonder what she is thinking.

"I must go," I say, "I need to let Mummy know I'm back. She'll be worrying about me." Karin holds my hand tighter than ever.

"I'm sorry, Ricky," she says, her voice gentle but her words blaring, "Your mother, she was terribly ill when we left for Laeso, and she, well, she never got better. She died, Ricky. Hundreds of people died in the town, while we were away on the island. If you had stayed, if we had stayed, we might have caught the same cruel disease." She takes a cloth from her sleeve and wipes tears from her eyes. "I am so sorry, darling."

I am numb but at once whisper, "I knew, really." I stare down through the window to the town far below. My eyes strain to spot mother's red cloak gliding along the harbourside or up the alleys leading to the castle. I try my hardest to detect her tender voice outside the chamber door. Then I remember my last sight of her, emaciated in the fever of her bed. I cling to Karin. She strokes my hair. I sob. I shall weep forever.

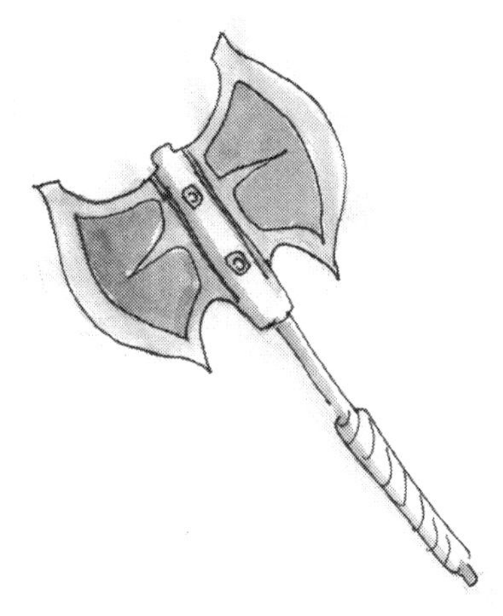

Chapter Five

Claudius

"One may smile, and smile, and be a villain;
At least I'm sure it may be so in Denmark"
[Hamlet I,v]

Another memory, this time from my twenties. Etched on my mind by not grief but terror.

The night is pitch black. I fear for my life. I am in mortal danger from someone eight years my junior. But no common seventeen year old. The youth I have offended is Prince Claudius.

Ever since the death in battle last week of the old King his father, Claudius has been spoiling for trouble. It is a strange way of mourning. His elder brother Hamlet, now the King, although his coronation has yet to happen, is not back from the war. When his ship reaches Elsinore the victory celebrations will be muted. True it is that old

Fortinbras the agelong thorn in Denmark's foot is slain and at Prince Hamlet's hand; but it is a cruel blow to the nation that our own King has fallen in the same conflict.

Claudius' reaction has been extreme. First he drew his rapier and threatened the messenger who had ridden many miles, as if murdering him might annul the news he bore. Perhaps he hates the idea that his brother will now take the crown. Then he summoned a knot of his friends, a group of the more pugnacious young courtiers. With them he has brawled and bullied the nights away in the taverns. Tonight they ended up in the Great Hall with some girls they had rounded up in the town. The Prince called for me to entertain this rabble. When I sent the message that I was sick, he dispatched three heavy-handed companions to fetch me. I had no option but to obey.

The atmosphere was hardly conducive to skilful clowning. Those rowdies were more interested in mocking me than appreciating any niceties of verbal and physical wit. When I delivered a precise and graceful cartwheel, some buffoon proposed a tumbling contest, the prize to be a roll in the straw with the youngest of the girls, a pretty maid of about fourteen who was clearly frightened at this turn of events. I felt sorry for her and resolved to win the competition and engineer her escape. If only it had been that simple.

Needless to say, despite my executing the most perfect routine of somersaults and extended handstands, the prize went to Claudius through the acclaim of his drunken cronies. I glanced at the girl. A frail creature, she was in tears. We both knew that she would suffer rough treatment from the Prince. I stepped forward.

"My Lord Claudius," I called out, "Allow me to enhance your pleasure! This maid's coarse apparel is scarce fit for a swineherd's consort, let alone that of a Royal Prince. I have among my store of costumes a selection of silken undergarments brought from France. They are, one might rightly say, of a 'revealing' nature. They will create of her a feast for your majesty's eyes as well as your other senses. May I thus 'prepare' her accordingly, for your delectation?"

At this suggestion the mob let out a salacious roar. Claudius smirked, looking round for approval in the faces of his companions. "Why not?" he answered, "But keep your dirty great hands off her, d'yer hear, you oaf!"

"Of course, your majesty," I said with an obsequious bow, "In fact, so that you may be sure that I resist the temptation to fondle the pretty little maid myself, why don't her friends come to help her dress. They'll be more skilled than I in draping the silken slips, preparing her, as a bride on her first night." I accompanied this with an obscene gesture of complicity, at which the louts burst into ribald laughter.

"Just hurry up," he snapped, "I'm getting horny for it." His cronies bellowed coarse wisecracks as I ushered all the girls from the hall.

The loutish youths are less amused now, an hour later, after realising that we have no intention of returning. All the maidens are safe in their own anonymous homes, but Claudius knows exactly where I live. The whole of Elsinore knows 'The Jester's House' in a side street beneath the palace wall. So even now his ruffians are beating on my barred door. Driven on by the wrath of the Prince, they mean me no good. I fear that my impertinence could cost me my life. This gang is known to have kicked to death a poor soldier who unwittingly offended one of their number.

I cower in the unlit room as they bay for my blood. The drunken shouts get louder. I hear someone calling for a battleaxe to hack down the door. I cannot control my trembling. There is no back door, no way of escape. Soon I hear the thud of the axe biting into wood. I remember Father Gregory and wish that after all I had chosen the protected life of a friar. If only English Crispin had survived that shipwreck and was still our court jester.

With the chopping, the clamour grows ever more raucous as they bellow for my surrender. I shrink into the chimney corner, but there is no hope now. The splintering timber of my door groans in sympathy with my despair. "Nearly there!" someone shouts. I say a Hail Mary. I think of the King and wish I were one of his guards rather than a pathetic jester. At least then I should have been capable of putting up a fight. The door yields. A blood-curdling screech. Then another shout goes up, different in tone and farther off. The sound of retreating footfalls. Followed by an ominous silence.

It must be a trick. A villain's ruse to raise my hope of escape before I am seized. I remain still, crouched among the cold ashes of the hearth, listening to the desperate beating of my heart. But what's this? A different rhythm. Marching boots, tramping up the cobbled street towards my battered door. Claudius must have organised reinforcements to take me, I surmise. And then the tread of boots marches past the house, up Castle Hill.

A voice rings out. My next door neighbour. "The King!" he shouts, "Long live King Hamlet!" Others join in. Soon the street is echoing with the same excited cry. The young King is home. I have survived.

But I have made an enemy.

Chapter Six

Love of my Life

"'Tis brief, my lord."
"As woman's love."
[Hamlet, III, ii]

My journal from here on was intermittent. Then this momentous entry, a few years later:

She came today from over the sea. Her ship was decked in the gayest bunting, which fluttered in a gentle breeze while the summer sun shone down to bless her arrival. Her face veiled, her slender form draped in virginal gossamer, she sat erect on a delicate gilt throne between the rowers. A faery princess! With proud solemnity her father, the Swedish monarch, led her by the hand over a carpetted gangway to the quay, where the young King Hamlet waited, his guard of honour and velvet-robed

Cabinet of Ministers behind him. Further back stood lesser courtiers, myself included, while most of Elsinore's citizens lined the far reach of the harbour wall to witness her coming.

It was a magical moment. The wind dropped. Stillness. We were all silent, entranced, under her spell. Every eye was on her as the King went down on one knee and murmured some words of welcome. He then rose, turned his face to the people and with a regal sweep of the arm presented to us our future Queen.

The crowds erupted with wild cheering which continued for a quarter-hour as the royal procession, flanked by ceremonial guards, wended its way to the castle. Then we dispersed, I to prepare for the evening's feast of welcome.

Her beauty is extraordinary, magnetic. At the banquet, even happily-married dignitaries like Polonius kept glancing her way. Claudius could not take his eyes off her as she sat graceful and demure between the two Kings, her father and her husband-to-be. For my own part, although I knew that King Hamlet wanted me to share my tomfoolery with everyone throughout the hall, I was constantly drawn to where she sat. She the candle, I the doomed moth. Distracted by her nearness, I performed badly. I fumbled a coin which should have appeared from the Chancellor's ear. Luckily it landed on his platter and I contrived to recover it while pretending to wipe gravy from his beard, with a napkin containing a bright blue dye. He was a self-important fellow and as I glided away I could hear the roar of laughter from those around him who could see his woaded face. I glanced back at the Princess. Her green eyes were on me and my heart hit the roof. First her smile, then her following look!

Concentrating on my work, I pell-melled to the door. Once in the courtyard I clambered into my jousting-horse, grabbed my wooden sword and galloped back into the hall. And, oh God, she was watching the doorway as she listened to the King. I made my idiotic mount rear up in fright then away I galumphed around the hall as though he had bolted. I struggled to control the frantic creature, up and down between the long tables, as I bellowed Whoa There and Help! Finally the beast was calm and I came to a breathless halt. Where else but right beside her. God help me, I could not do otherwise.

She turned her face to me. Close up she is divine. Her skin so pure. And she was laughing at my act. Ecstacy. She rose to her feet and all the men in the hall did so too, even the King. Reaching out, she took from my shaking hands the reins of my steed. I was helpless. My heart a frightened dove in a cage. My face an independent creature, grinning uncontrollably.

She caressed Dobbin's muzzle and mimed feeding him a sweetmeat. "There, there," she whispered. Her voice was adorable, that Swedish lilt. "Let's get you to your stable." Calmly, under the awed eyes of the whole court, she walked me by the reins, back to the shadowed doorway. The revellers broke into respectful applause, but I was only half aware of that, for before she released me her hand touched mine. Lightly, briefly – but intentionally? And then …

"Where is Dobbin's stable?" she asked in a murmur.

"Castle Hill. The green shutters. On the right."

"Tomorrow. After dark." Did she really say it? The King's bride?

I heard further clapping when she returned to the hall. I stood bemused for a long moment, then cantered my ridiculous hack out to the yard.

I was lost.

The impossible came true. She came to my door. Late in the evening. I was watching through a chink in my shutter, saw the flutter of her cloak in the moonlight. Her furtive flit down the hill. The backward glance to check she was not followed, before she crossed the street.

I let her in, my heart threatening to explode. Behind her I dropped into its slots the heavy stanchion that would hold my door against all intruders. Turning to enfold her I pressed my lips to hers. They were cool and velvet soft. Neither of us spoke. The mystery of our shared compulsion needed no words.

A thousand times since, I have relived that night. I take her cloak. Beneath it she wears a kitchenmaid's rough shift, borrowed for her secret escape from the castle. It smells still of the grease of roasting boar, an aroma evermore evocative for me. I lead her by the hand to the deep bearskin lying before the fire. We kneel face to face as if in a silent prayer of thanksgiving for this pure joy. Her elfin features shine in the flickering light. She smiles her radiance and I know that in my insuppressible beaming she recognises my soul's rapture. I shall remember this moment with my dying breath.

Solemn, we kiss again. Our mouths linger, savouring the sweetness of forbidden pleasure. Then with simultaneous intent we fumble to lift from her the coarse tunic. I am a gauche boy once more, stripped of all the facile dexterity of my much-practiced seduction technique.

Clad now in the royal silk only of her underdress, she is once more a princess. She lies back on the fur. My eyes luxuriate in the draped contours of her body and I am awestruck. Never among my many conquests have I been ravished so. She lifts her hands to offer her embrace. She draws me down to lie over her. Her legs are parted and mine fit snug between them. With a sigh she folds smooth arms about my neck.

My urgent desires kindled, I jump up, strip off my shirt. I loose the strings of my doublet and kick it aside. Its buckle clinks against the canikin of wine, the best I could coax from the King's kitchener. I fill two beakers.

When I turn back she is naked. She lies on her belly, her face towards me. Firelight illuminates the texture and shape of her body. Her mischievous green eyes dwell on her first sight of my man's parts, which are certainly in no state of repose. I put the drinks aside, releasing my hands to cover my embarrassment. Why? My male prowess has always hitherto been proud to display itself. She laughs. I adore the warmth and languor of her laughter. Oh, I enjoy inducing the mirth of the young

King. But paradise comes when I know that she is the one I please.

Now I crouch at her side. She purrs like a housecat as I in wonder trace the outline of her spine. Her back arches to meet my fingers. It is longer than I imagined, her hips more shapely, her skin more miraculous. I gaze down on her, loth to move closer, as an explorer might hesitate to defile the temple in some new-discovered land.

She rolls on one side, her back to the fire. For the first time I survey the mystical beauty of these youthful breasts. Gravely she smiles as she takes my hand. She places a soft kiss in its palm, then draws it to stroke across, one by one, her nipples. They nuzzle into my hand, which curves to caress the one while I bend to kiss the other. The intensity of her stare into my eyes is magnetic, the excitement in the contact between her flesh and mine delectable.

A puny voice in my head tells me to desist from such madness. But the momentum of my, of *our* desire is remorseless. My hands, my mouth are let loose on the divinity of her royal body. They reconnoitre her cheeks, nose and lips; the whiteness of her neck, her shoulders, arms and hands. They visit again those breasts, even more alive now with the quickening of her breath. They explore the musky mysteries that hide beneath her soft maidenly tuft.

Catching my urgency, she pulls me down on her, arms and legs wrapt about me. And in the transport of the communion of our beings – bodies, minds and very souls – we enter the ecstasy to which nothing could have admitted us, other than our coming together.

We are at one. Yorick – and Gertrude.

Chapter Seven

Prince Hamlet

"Here hung those lips that I have kissed
I know not how oft."
[Hamlet, V, i]

The meaning of despair. I came to know it all too soon, long before the birth of Queen Gertrude's baby. It was so clear that she and the King were happy together and I condemned to say goodbye forever to the bliss of love. Did I but dream that we had given ourselves to each other with such complete and joyful abandon? And was it possible that when, before the first light of the next day she slipped unnoticed back into the castle, she left the memory of her visit behind her, never again to think of it?

During the royal wedding and the festivities which followed, did she glance at me? Not once! Immaculately the perfect bride, she clung to King Hamlet's arm so that all the world would believe she adored him utterly. Wretched, I obeyed my cue. In the celebrations I was the perfect jester. Ha! Perfect, yes, even to the cliche of bottling up my secret tears, just as the tragic clown is expected to do. Oh, the laughter I raised with my quips and tricks! The gasps of amazement I extracted from those who watched my sleights of hand! But I kept my distance from Gertrude and whenever I stole a look at her she would be deep in conversation with the King or some nearby courtier.

Inevitably, this Spring, the paragon wife supplied King and Nation with a son and heir. Another Hamlet, Prince of Denmark! There was huge rejoicing in the land and, following the child's baptism, the most lavish banquet at which I of course was summoned to entertain. I could not bear to do it. In my place I sent my apprentice, a talented lad, with the message that I had a fever. The King kindly dispatched a servant bearing food and ale for me, to say that he and Queen Gertrude would miss me at the feast.

I stayed alone behind the green shutters with the ale and my broken heart.

After that I spent too much time with the bottle, though not always alone. Following one such evening I returned to my journal:

The wall that jumped up to hit me was hard against my cheek. Very hard. Hard, and sharp too. So I decided to lie there a while until the world stopped spinning. My face was bleeding. My bladder fit to burst. My belly too full.

First things first, I thought. So I threw up. I tried to keep my legs apart so that the mixture of ale and bile and herring and cheap wine from the tavern wouldn't end up all over my boots. Unsuccessfully. But so what, I knew the rain would wash them clean. Especially if I walked home in the gutter down the middle of the street. There was a fair old torrent gushing down the hill.

I got to my feet by holding onto the wall, then noticed I was pissing. Inside my doublet. Better out than in, as English Crispin used to say. The wet felt warm and comforting on the skin of my legs. I decided to lean against the wall for a while before heading home. My face was wet. Was it rain or blood? Never mind, I remember thinking, the blood'll wash the rain away.

The evening hadn't begun like that. It was going to be different from last week, when I made a fool of myself with some Dutch sailors at the drinking house. Three nights running. Tonight was going to be the new, the pulling-himself-together Yorick. The Yorick who didn't accidently fall over during a royal banquet (they laughed. They thought it was deliberate). But then I went to the tavern. Just to be sociable. One quick cup of Canary wine then home for supper and an early night!

What happened was, I bumped into a couple of pals who were celebrating something or other. I forget what. Oh yes, I remember now, the young one, he's been in work for exactly two years without a break. I asked him how he knew it was the exact date and he said he'd started the job the very day young Prince Hamlet was born. Whenever he hears the celebration birthday bells of the royal chapel ringing out, he checks which month and if it's April he knows. So he puts away his pick and shovel and heads for the tavern.

"Pick and shovel?" I asked.

"That's right. I'm the number two gravedigger down at the cemetery. Have a drink!"

So I did. And then another. Just to be sociable. And after a couple more, I sang him my song about being dead and buried – 'In Youth when I did Love, did Love' – and he liked it so much I taught it him there and then. Then we sang it together, and a couple more ballads. It was getting to be a merry old night. I hailed the landlord for another flagon of wine and turned to my young pal.

"You'll be alright, then," I said, "when you kick the bucket."

"How d'you mean?"

"Well, won't you get a free plot at the graveyard?"

"No such luck." He shook his head sadly.

"Why so glum?"

"Ah," he sighed, "When I think of all the good and the not so good folk I've housed in their graves, yet for me there'll be no Christian burial in the hallowed ground."

"Why not?"

"Why, for the fact that I was denied the Holy Baptism an infant should receive, on account of my Mam being a slave brought from a heathen land."

"Oh, is that all," I answered, "We can put that little matter right, here and now." I leapt onto the table, snatched up the flagon and emptied the wine over his head, making the sign of the cross and shouting out, "I name this child Dave Grigger, in the name of his father. God bless him and all who quaff ale with him!"

"Dave Grigger? What kind of a name is that?" he asked as he sat there dripping with Rhenish, and joining the laughter which rang around him.

"Well," I said, "There's no such name in the world as Grave Digger!"

Then we sang our song again. Then I ordered another flagon and helped drink it. Just to be sociable. And after he and the sexton had gone home I ordered one more, which I drank alone. Because it was the Prince's second birthday. And because I couldn't forget my night with his mother.

I don't know when I ate the pickled herring.

When did I get control of my drinking? It was two years later. I can recall the day.

Queen Gertrude had summoned me (did my heart leap or sink? Certainly it jolted) to the sideroom where she spent most of her days with Prince Hamlet, already four years old. The King was away with an army, fighting the Poles on a frozen Baltic shore. My knees wobbled as I reached the door. A nurse admitted me, then bowed before leaving. Gertrude was sat on a cushion before the fire, watching the flames. The little Prince slept on a deep rug in the corner. I hesitated by the door.

"Come in, sit over here." She had almost lost her Swedish accent, but the voice still gave me that involuntary thrill. It was the first time I had been alone with her since. Since, well, you know when.

With a "Thank you, your Majesty!" I took a stool at the far side of the hearth. She nodded, but kept her eyes on the fire. I was longing to receive the gift of her smile. I wanted to run away from there, I wanted to stay for ever. The silence was endless, agonising for me. I had to break it. My voice cracked as I spoke.

"You sent for me, Majesty?"

"I did, Yorick." Without turning her head, she sighed. I ached to have her look into my face with those pellucid eyes. After a further silence she went on, "I want you to ..." her words faded away. Then with a deep breath she found new resolution.

"I want you to teach Hamlet some of your tricks."

I was bewildered. So much so that for one wild moment I imagined she meant the King, and that the tricks she meant were those of the bedroom. Then I realised. She was talking of the young Prince.

"Do you think, Yorick, that he might have any aptitude? Would he enjoy learning rhymes and songs and simple conjuring spells?"

"I am sure he would, Majesty, though he is young. He is a bright boy, a quick learner. I shall make it fun for him."

"Then see to it. Come to him in the mornings. The nurse will stay with you both, to help if needed." At last she stood as I had, and turned to face me. My heart lurched. She smiled, but I could not. Reaching out, she rested a hand on my shoulder. I met her eyes. They were as green, as beautiful as ever. I searched them for the passion I'd once known in them. They were neutral.

"Are you happy to do it?"

"I am more than happy."

"Tomorrow morning, then."

"Yes, Majesty." I made a move to leave but she stopped me with a word.

"There … there is one more thing."

"Your Highness?"

"I want you to know that I … I am perfectly happy now. Now, at last. It has taken most of these five years and dutiful devotion to the King my husband, for me to feel this way. Fortunately, he is the best, the kindest and bravest of men. My reward is the married bliss with which I now am blessed."

I was unable to look at her. I numbly watched the fire and imagined the flames of Hell. "Majesty?" I stammer. What else was there to say? With a glance at the door she continued, her voice lowered.

"There is one thing you, and only you in the world, should know." Again she paused. I waited. After a moment she said, "The King has accepted the fact that he can no longer father children. It is the result of an illness he suffered in his youth."

I was stunned. Why was she telling me this?

"He believes this infertility has come about since our marriage, that is ... subsequent to the ... to the genesis of the Prince. But ... but that is not the case."

I was staring at her in consternation. Distracted, she seemed to be concentrating on her clenched fists. A tear trickled down her cheek. I glanced across at the child. He slept on, his tiny face towards me. And then I noticed his eyebrows. Dear God, they were mine!

"Then Prince Hamlet is my ..." I began, but she interrupted.

"Do not say it! Never say it! I beg of you that you bury this secret in your heart, as I have done; at first as my queenly duty and now from the overwhelming love I bear my husband. He adores Prince Hamlet and nobody, not even you, my unforgettable Yorick, could be a more loving and devoted father."

Me, a devoted father? My mind went back to the two daughters I had sired in Halsingborg by two sisters during a State Visit there with the old King ten years before. What kind of a father was I to them? All I ever did was to respond to their grandfather's angry letter by sending them the contents of my purse. I didn't even know whether they were still alive. And then I dismissed them from my consciousness as I took in the words Gertrude had just used. "Unforgettable? Unforgettable Yorick!"

A discreet knock at the door, and at the Queen's call the nurse returned. It was the end of my interview.

Gertrude explained to her that for an hour each morning the nurse and I would share the care of young Hamlet. For the first time, I registered this attendant. She was Swedish, a little on the plump side and decidedly pretty. Next to the Queen, however, she was ordinary.

At that moment the Prince woke up and tottered sleepily to his mother. "You know Yorick, don't you? He's going to show you how to do some tricks," she said softly as he stood rubbing his eyes. I stepped forward and snatched the adorable boy up in my arms. Then I lifted him bodily in a twirl over my head to sit him astride my shoulders.

"Come on," I cried, "I'll be your horsey whenever you want a ride!" I cantered around the room while he crowed with pleasure. The happiness! My son! My unmentionable child!

Chapter Eight

Punishment

"I have not from your eyes that gentleness
And show of love that I was wont to have."
[Julius Caesar, I, ii]

My thirtieth birthday. I can never forget it. Fear, darkness, pain!

They came for me in the night. Bursting in through my unbolted door, they woke me and dragged me to the castle. Not through the main gate, that great arch which I had used daily for months on my way to tutor the Prince. Instead they frogmarched me stumbling to the depths of the keep. There they left me crouched against a clammy dungeon wall in the total dark until a grey dawn's wan light became visible through the bars of a grille high up in the rough stonework.

At first I thought this was Claudius' old grudge come home to roost, but when I demanded the reason for my arrest, the sergeant-at-arms was offhand.

"King's command, old son, that's all I know. The orders come down and I do as I'm told. That's how it works, mate, bishops or clowns, it's all the same to me. Mind you, you are in exceptionally deep shit. He's in a right lather. What you been up to, eh?" He didn't linger for a reply.

With the daylight came my first and only caller, attended by four guards. It was the King. I searched his face for the meaning of my imprisonment. His eyes, which I had a thousand times made smile, were full of hurt. Tight-lipped, he had me hustled by torchlight to a narrower windowless cell where he ordered the men to shackle me then to wait in the guardroom. He stayed, sat on the bare wooden bench opposite where I crouched doubled up against the wall. The damp air stank of stale sweat and piss. I stared at the ground.

"I should have you killed." He hissed. I had never heard his voice like this, heavy with menace. "I should kill you myself." He was wringing his hands. For a moment I was afraid he would strangle me there and then, yet I pitied his torment. How terrible, I thought, if this good man, this King Hamlet whom I have known and loved all his life, should be reduced to a common executioner. Then I remembered to worry about myself. I had my problems, yet had no wish to die. Not on my birthday. If I had been meant to die young, the pestilence would have taken me with my mother. Or perhaps I should have perished with my mentor old Crispin when his ship foundered on the Jutland coast. But not here, please God! Not now!

I heard myself speak, hardly recognising my own

voice which was no more than a parched croak.

"Your Majesty, I do not understand." I raised my face to plead with him. He would not look at me.

"It is treason, Yorick, treason!"

"Treason, my lord? I have ever been your loyal subject. I swear it." The convincing affirmation I intended came out as a tremulous mumble, such was my terror.

"Treason!" he repeated, "And the punishment for treason against the King is death."

I threw myself at his feet. The shackle cut into my leg. "Your Majesty, help me to understand!"

Seizing the hair at the back of my neck, he thrust his face up close. His eyes were as full of grief as anger. "The Prince." His voice was flat with helpless resignation.

"Prince Hamlet?" My mind whirled. Had harm come to the boy and I been blamed? "I would never, never hurt him. I love him as if he were my own!"

The words were scarce off my tongue when I realised. He knew. The King knew. With a swing of his fist he knocked me flat. My mouth filled with blood from a loosened tooth. He stood above me. He was going to kick me to death. But no blows came. Instead he seized my shoulder and heaved me to my feet. He stood before me, man to man. There was steel in his expression.

"Yorick, many men would call me fool for not having you put to death. But, Heaven help me, I try to be a man of my word. The Queen …" he hesitated, emotion clogging his words, "The Queen and I, in our deep devotion to each other – a devotion you shall never experience, I pity you for it – have unveiled, and forgiven, all secrets between us. All secrets. Including you. Including … my son!"

For a moment he seemed unable to speak on. In the silence he was staring into my face. Then, with a calmness that was truly royal, he added, "I have promised the Queen, out of my love for her, to be merciful to you, and so I shall be. On this morning's tide a merchant vessel sets sail from Elsinore, bound for England. You shall be aboard. You will never return to Denmark."

Overwhelmed with relief and humility, I began to thank him. "Your Majesty …"

"The justification for your banishment, the court will learn, is your persistent pilfering from the royal wine cellar, the which I knew of long ago, although I am aware that it has not happened of late. In this way, the good name of the Queen will be protected; and the Prince shall remain my beloved son and the heir to Denmark's throne."

I fell to my knees and kissed his feet in fealty and gratitude. My eyes were swamped with tears. With one last look of pity, of loathing, of regret, he strode from the cell.

Chapter Nine

Cawdor

"Confusion now hath made his masterpiece."
[Macbeth, II, iii]

After my sudden expulsion from Denmark it was many months before I resumed my journal:

I thank my fate to have reached a haven here in the Duke of Albany's court. I little thought such good fortune possible when a few short weeks ago I found myself alone and sheltering from a blizzard beneath the ruins of a great wall. The locals, in their peculiar dialect had told me this ancient relic was once ordered by a Roman emperor (no doubt to exclude from his empire the likes of my previous master).

That snow! We had snow a'plenty at Elsinore but not this

wet and heavy British variety, textured like the 'porridge' I was forced to eat for the last several months. I thank God that I headed south.

When the Lark dropped me on the Scottish coast last summer I was mightily relieved. Throughout the five day voyage from Denmark the crew had eyed me sideways. King Hamlet had paid them to take me to my exile but once at sea I was merely another mouth to feed. And as the weather turned savage they openly accused me of being a jinx. Had the captain not been a devout Christian I should most likely have been tossed overboard. As it was, he took the first opportunity to put me ashore with nothing but the ragged clothes I stood in.

Picture my desolation! I was in a strange land, the waves lapping at my feet as I surveyed a seemingly endless spread of sand. It was dawn. From the direction of the sun I noted that this was a north-facing coast. Searching the horizon for signs of habitation I made out a plume of smoke far off. I trudged in that direction, driven by hunger to ignore all imagined dangers.

The fire which drew me belonged to a humble farmer who gave me shelter in his turf-clad croft. His wife scurried about preparing food for me – a local 'delicacy' known as hag's eye or some such name. Formed from a beast's belly, it would have been deemed unfit for the King of Denmark's hogs, let alone his servants. Still, I was in no fit state to quibble. In truth I

believe that by his lights (apt term!) he was treating me royally. Certainly his seven open-jawed children watched with envious eyes as I consumed the feast. They rewarded me with shy smiles of gratitude when I contrived to slip a sliver to each of them.

After some hours' sleep I learned from my host that the nearest town was several leagues distant and was called Forres. What was more, the Scottish King was rumoured to be in the vicinity. This news was welcome. It held out the possibility of employment. What kind of royal court could survive without a jester? Ha! This I was to discover before the year was out.

As soon as I could decently do so, I bade a grateful farewell to the crofter and his family. My intention was to introduce myself to the Royal household. However, on reaching Forres I found that the King, Duncan, was encamped outside the town in order to save the townspeople from the risk of slaughter in battle. For I had arrived in a country riven with civil strife. To the south a rebel force loomed, outnumbering the royal cohorts. Worse, Denmark's old enemy Norway was supporting the insurgents with a great army let by the warlike King Sweno. When I learnt this from a sentry at the camp, my heart sank. Had I been spared in my homeland only to fall into the hands of the merciless Norseman?

What I should have realised was that my alien accent would awaken the guard's suspicion. He kept me in conversation until a comrade arrived, whereupon he seized me. I was dragged before the King and denounced as a spy. Before I had the opportunity to plead my innocence, however, there was a dramatic interruption. A bloody-headed soldier galloped into the camp, fell from his foaming horse and was helped into the royal presence.

Once he had his breath back, this fellow began to recount, in what I thought to be an unnecessarily convoluted manner, the news from the battlefield. It seemed that things were going surprisingly well for the loyalists. Duncan was cheered by this but sobered up when another messenger, a Thane this time, arrived to inform him that the Norwegians and rebels had started to knock 'our' people cold. However, it seemed that this Thane too had the national habit of making the most of a good story. In the next breath he reported that all was well. Some captain (who evidently was due to marry a woman called Bella or it might have been Bellona), having killed the chief traitor, had almost single-handed forced Sweno to surrender.

Great celebrations ensued in the castle at Forres. Duncan, a sweet and trusting King, accepted my account of how I'd been shipwrecked (I felt it impolitic to go into the business of my banishment). I was given dry clothes and boots and invited to share in the festivities. The highpoint of these was the arrival of the all-conquering hero, called Macbeth, and his right hand man Banquo. The two had been honoured with new thanedoms and were welcomed with wild cheering. However, the longest applause came when the King announced that his eldest son Malcolm would be Prince of Cumberland and heir to the throne. Nobody clapped louder than Macbeth but I noticed that his smile was a little forced. At the time I wondered whether he was carrying a wound of some sort. Later I was to realise that whatever injury he bore was a mental one which had fatally affected his very human kindness.

I could see that the party at Forres was my opportunity. Before the night was out I had the thanes and earls and princes rolling in the aisles as they say. Despite my fatigue, and fuelled by the generous amounts of an amber liquor which was freely on offer, I delivered one of the merriest performances of my life. So much so that when the King and Court yawningly reassembled the following afternoon I was invited to travel with the royal party as official Fool. We were destined for Macbeth's castle at Inverness.

Jesters in a Scottish royal establishment clearly come low in the staff pecking order. Next day I was left behind at the camp outside Forres as the King, his Thanes, their ladies and senior servants processed across the hills to Macbeth's stronghold. Together with the lower ranks, I was to help tidy the site before following on later that week. It was typical of Duncan that he wished to save local residents the inconvenience of cleaning up the mess and ordure an army leaves in its wake. I was looking forward to serving such a king. It was not to be.

After a day's filthy toil we set out. We endured a nightmare trek through continual rainstorms, a forced march so that we could catch up with the royal party. Under the command of an officer called Seyton, a sinister fellow (my fellow toilers referred to him as Satan), we were driven like cattle along muddy drovers' trails, stopping only once to take a scarcely edible meal of oatcake and salted venison strips. There was something ominous too about Culloden, the village where we halted, a grim cluster of low cottages cowering against a barren hillside as if awaiting a nightmare fate. The place did nothing to brighten my feelings about the journey. It was hell. Or so I thought at the time. Worse was to come.

But not immediately. We reached Inverness as the evening sun broke through, shortly after the arrival of the Royal household. The very sight of the Castle against an azure sky cheered me. Martins wheeled from every battlement in the delicate air. And smoke rising from the chimneys spoke of warm lodgings and hot meals to come. And then the resumption of my jesting career.

Seyton had other ideas. "You," he shouted across the courtyard, "Yes you, the one who thinks he's so funny."

I peered at the other dozen or so exhausted fellows as if to spot who he could possibly have meant.

"Yes, you, the ginger-nut, the Norwegian!"

I pointed to myself in mock disbelief.

"Don't push your luck with me or you'll wish you'd stayed in whatever cave you crawled out of. I've got a job for you."

"Whatever you say, your majesty," I replied. The irony was lost on him.

"You're manning the South Gate for the night. Starting now! The rest of you rabble can stand down. There's food and plenty of drink in the messroom. Courtesy of the Thane of Cawdor."

"What, the traitor?" said one of the men, "I thought he was dead."

"Not him, you bumpkin. The new Cawdor, of course. The lord Macbeth!"

So it was that, while my comrades took their leisure where the venison roasted and the liquors flowed free, I was exiled to act as porter at the south entry of the castle. However, my dismay was mollified a half-hour later when two of these friends came to me bearing a board of meat and a large flagon. The former satisfied my belly but the latter went straight to my head. When I awoke my ears were throbbing. Or so I thought. In fact the knocking which assailed my brain came from the gate. Yet I was inebriated to the degree that at first I imagined it came from within me and that I was back among my compatriots, making them laugh with a series of what at the time I believed great witticisms. How drink deceives us! As the knocking continued I maintained my fanciful stream of jokes about being the keeper of hell's gate. It wasn't far from the grisly truth.

Within minutes of my admitting the Lord Macduff, Inverness Castle was in uproar. Duncan, that gentle King was found dead: murdered in his bed by drunken servingmen, presumed to be in the pay of the defeated rebel leader. Macbeth, in his grief and rage, hacked the killers to pieces on the spot. The Princes, Malcolm and young Donalbain, fled in panic and were, it was announced, suspected of joining the rebel-rousing remnants of the Norwegian army

Macbeth warned everyone to be on guard against any such treachery. He put the whole region on a war footing and within a week, in the absence of any overt objection, accepted the cowed thanes' invitation to assume the crown. Without delay he took his retinue to a place called Scone or Stone, where tradition demanded the Scottish King be invested.

Meanwhile, what of poor Yorick? My duties now were never those of a jester. I was porter, waiter, kennelman, whatever task was needed as one by one Macbeth's old servants deserted his fortress. Most of them were alienated by the new King's rages, some by his Lady's increasing madness. And all found it impossible to work with Macbeth's right-hand man, Seyton, whose stock had risen as the elder courtiers had left. Like the others I too took to calling him Satan. Indeed, many said this name was closer to the truth about that sinister man. As Macbeth's rule became more and more a reign of terror, with murder and pillage rife in the land, I sought the means to escape. Soon after the death of the Queen I was again placed on duty at the south portal. When all was quiet I opened the gate and took my leave of Dunsinane. And once I'd crossed the ancient Roman wall I found myself in that part of England known as the Dukedom of Albany.

Chapter Ten

Vocation

"We have seen the best of our time: machinations, hollowness, treachery, and all ruinous disorders follow us disquietly to our graves."
[King Lear, I,ii]

Three years passed. It was a time in which my fortunes waxed and waned until in desperation I came to seek fulfilment in what as a youth I had rejected. I wrote of this while in heavy seas off England's coast.

God forgive me that I have so long spurned my true vocation. I have taken on me the humble cloak of penitence and accept with resignation my present discomfort amidst the waves which churn with the Lord's displeasure. The French King's vessel is a fragile cockleshell as we ride out the storm with sails furled. Should it be granted to us that we reach Calais, I shall commit myself to the life of poverty and service which the blessed Francis of Assisi himself espoused. Can it really be more than twenty-five years since Father Gregory first spoke to me of such an existence? And almost as long a time since I rejected its strictures and its treasures in favour of my self-serving life in the Danish court?

I am done with fooling. England has crushed out of me all the wit and zest I once would put into my work. Although by God's good grace I am still alive, the jester in me is dead.

On my arrival in England, fate smiled on me. I made good use of my past links with old Crispin, whose lingering reputation secured me introductions to the court. Moreover, his tutelage in the language now proved invaluable. By the end of the first summer I had employment as jester to Albany, son-in-law to the King himself. The Duchess being a great one for feasts and entertainments, I had ample opportunity to display my skill in clowning and to hone my facility with the English tongue – one which provides ridiculous scope for wordplay. In short, I became a favourite in Albany's entourage.

This applied in particular, I am now ashamed to confess, to the Duchess, the Princess Goneril. My verbal trickery was of little interest to her but from the first she was drawn by my agility. I became aware that she was rivetted by my somersaults and back-flips. When I doubled over backwards and walked crabwise across the floor, she would be watching my body with an unusual intensity. It came therefore as little surprise when one day she summoned me to her suite. The Duke was away, engaged in some tour of his estates. What did astound me was the directness of her approach. As soon as I had closed the door behind me she said, "I have never before had a fool. Except for the Duke, of course!"

With that she rose and came to me. She allowed the gown to slip from her shoulders, revealing a magnificence of body which no man, let alone a longtime celibate such as I then was, could ignore. She was every inch a king's daughter!

There ensued what was in all senses an exhausting night, the first of many in the months that followed. When she learnt that she could rely on my discretion as well as my physical prowess, she took every opportunity to gain pleasure from the tone which my gymnastics maintained.

Two developments brought this clandestine episode to a close. First, there arrived at the castle a young man named Edmund. He was a plausible enough fellow with handsome features, although there was about him something of the night. Perhaps this was what appealed to Goneril for soon afterwards she lost interest in me. It was a relief. I had become more and more concerned that the Duke, poor chap, might learn of his wife's infidelities and have me disposed of. In truth I would have extricated myself sooner had she not threatened me in veiled but unmistakable terms with a fate of that sort. Jesters are politically expendable.

The presence of Edmund benefitted me in another way too. Soon after his arrival, the King's Fool, a young chap, took ill and died. My own professional reputation having reached the ears of the court, I was sent for. Albany was reluctant to let me go. Her Ladyship was all too eager to have me out of the way.

Thus it befell that I became Fool to Lear, King of England (or, as in his dotage he preferred to be addressed, of Britain).

I loved King Lear. With him I became like an old man's dog, plodding everywhere in his wake. There was less call for my athleticism, which was some relief as, having reached the age of forty, I no longer boasted the slim build of my youth. Lear relished it best when I took verbal liberties as the all-licensed Fool of the Royal Court, mocking obsequious hangers-on and aiming my satirical jibes at those who fawned on his favours. In this way I made friends of those loyal to the King and enemies of the false-hearted lords who were feathering their own nests.

Those were happier days, before the King's madness took hold. It began with the division of the Nation. What a catastrophe! I could understand his wishing to announce the dowry he intended for gentle Cordelia in order to secure her a marriage to the French King or the powerful Duke of Burgundy. But to dissect the state into three realms, each too weak to withstand a determined foe! Then, making matters worse, on a hot-headed whim to exclude his youngest and most worthy daughter! Such action flew in the face of all wisdom, even were the elder Princesses worthy to govern, for their husbands clearly lacked the backbone to stand up to those harpies. I feared the worst.

And so it transpired. Within the year my poor Nuncle was destitute, while Goneril and Regan rivalled each other for the title Queen of Heartlessness. For me, wit and jesting turned to bitter aloes on my tongue. Every attempted quip sounded to my ear like arid ranting. I could not stop. Instead of helping my master forget the source of his grief and savage regret, I would endlessly and uselessly revisit his folly. I hated myself. I pitied him.

As King Lear's own lunacy and self-contempt spiralled, so I perceived that I was of no use to him. At the first merciful opportunity I slipped away. We had been forced to abandon even the primitive comforts of a farmhouse whither the good Earl of Kent had led the King, along with Tom, a wretched idiot we had encountered sheltering naked in a hovel next the wintry heath. Our weary trudge towards Dover took us by the Greyfriars' Abbey at Winchelsea. There I remained. And in that holy haven my old calling to the monastic life was rekindled.

After I had ensured safe escort for the demented King I made my farewells and committed myself to the sage Franciscan Abbot of the place. He has armed me with credentials commending me to the Prior of a Monastery in the Italian hills of Umbria. Thither am I now intended, should the Good Lord in his mercy deliver us from this tempest. I fear we may all be drowned.

No matter what shall befall me, I pray that Heaven may protect my old Nuncle and restore to him both his Kingdom and his senses!

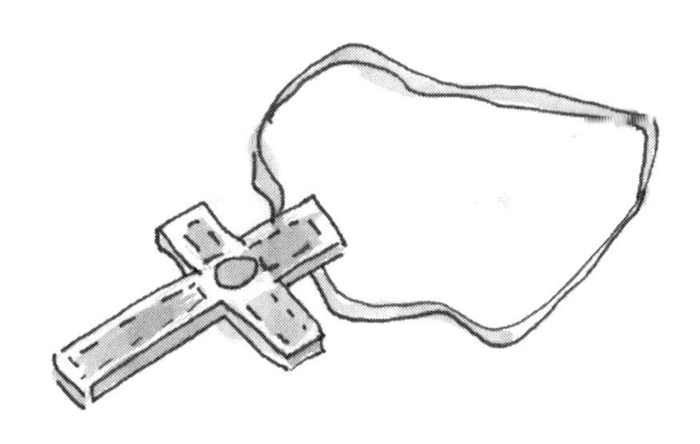

Chapter Eleven

Helena and Bertram

"From women's eyes this doctrine I derive:
They are the ground, the books, the academes,
From whence doth spring the true Promethian fire."
[Love's Labours Lost, IV, iii]

Well, we survived and with tattered sails made port at Calais. But what can I tell you of my journeyings thence to distant Assisi?

They began with good auspices. On landing I was fortunate to be befriended by a chaplain to the King of France. He secured me a place in the royal party at once returning to Paris. There I had time to compile a curriculum vitae recording my service in the courts of Denmark, Scotland and England (the services I rendered the Duchess of Albany I felt were better left untold). The King's First Lord was impressed. He became my advocate to His Majesty, which helped me to secure attendance in the palace and, later, a safe passage southward. However, this latter outcome came only after I had witnessed the most heart-lifting event followed by deeply unfitting behaviour by one at the Court.

It was no secret that the King had fallen victim to some dreadful disease whose remorseless progress now threatened his very life. Indeed, the court physicians had despaired of saving him. In his fever, he seemed even to have lost all recollection of his marriage to the fair Cordelia. He was resigned to a premature demise, which he was approaching with philosophical calm. He continued to rule with wisdom and equity, but the palace was imbued with a spirit of melancholy.

At this juncture there arrived in Paris a young woman called Helena. She claimed that rare prescriptions she had inherited from her late father would save the King. At first, weary of treatments and false hopes, he resisted her proposals. However, finally the blandishments of this most charming lady persuaded him to try her medications. Within a day, to everyone's astonishment, they had worked their magic. He was cured!

In profound gratitude the King granted her a boon. Her wish? To be married to a certain lord newly come to the Court, by name Bertram, Count of Rousillon. That 'gentleman' (I perjure myself by calling him such) in a distasteful show of snobbish disdain refused to take her to wife. The King insisted. Bertram pleaded. The King threatened. Bertram yielded. The couple were wed the same day.

Helena approached the ceremony with every evidence of fondest love in her adoring eyes. He by contrast bore an aloofness which bordered on hatred. The occasion would have been totally unpleasant had not the bride carried with her a joy and optimism which in the circumstances seemed truly unwarranted. In all it was hardly a happy start to a marriage and one held out no hope for its future. Misgivings increased when that very night the Count, instead of joining his besotted bride in bed, chose to depart for Florence. With him went his sidekick, a knavish braggart with the reputation of a coward.

Bertram's aim was to seek glory in the wars then sputtering in Tuscany, a conflict in which the French King had already taken steps to support his cousin the Duke of Florence. The following day emissaries were sent from Paris to meet with that lord. At my request I was given a place in their party, happy to serve in menial roles as long as it took me nearer my destination.

We reached Florence a week later to find callow Bertram established as General of Horse. I was saddened to learn that this newly-married fellow was already in course of wooing a local beauty, who prudently remained immune to his approaches. Frailty, thy name is woman? I think not. I only hope to Heaven that he will one day come to his senses and appreciate his loving wife's exceptional virtues. I pray that all will end well and that the labours of Helena's love are properly rewarded.

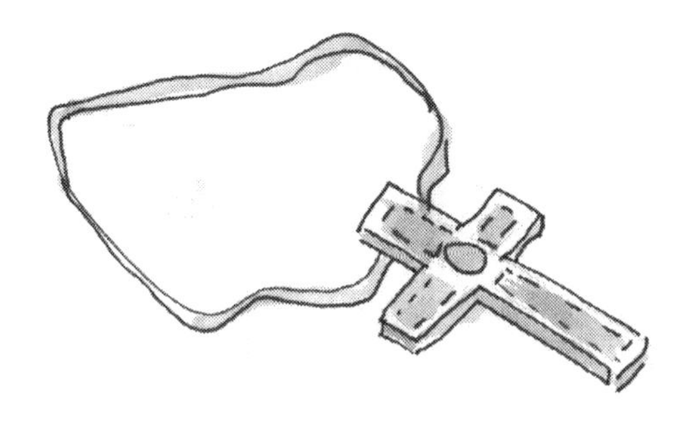

Chapter Twelve

Assisi

"I have ever lov'd the life remov'd,
And held in idle price to haunt assemblies
Where youth, and cost, and witless bravery keeps."
[Measure for Measure, I, iii]

But whether that may be so I shall never know. For within a day I left the French lords and took the dusty road to Perugia and thence at last to the home of the Little Brothers of St Francis. My pilgrimage to Assisi was complete. But the welcome I received was a surprise.

Ignatius was his name. I was ushered into a dusty crypt underneath the half-constructed basilica. There at a rough-hewn table sat the tallest man I had ever seen. He was also marked out by eyes which seemed to penetrate one's very thoughts. This was Ignatius, disciple of the Blessed Francis and custodian of the dead saint's manner of living. He was said to have the total confidence of the Holy Father in Rome as well as being the ascetic inheritor of Francis' love of the poor and humble. Here was one to whose way of life I aspired with all my heart.

It shocked me therefore when Brother Ignatius sent me away within a week of my arrival. The interview went like this.

"I understand your name is Yorick. And that you have travelled from the distant province of Denmark."

"That is so. I came indirectly, of course. Several years have passed since I departed the court at Elsinore."

"What has taken you so long to reach us? I understand that you sense a calling to join the Little Brothers and to serve the poor."

"I don't 'sense' this vocation. It is real. I first heard the voice twenty-five years ago, as a youth."

"And yet at that time you rejected it. In favour of what? What life's work drew you from this calling?"

"I … I became a jester. A performer at the court of …"

"I am aware of a jester's function, Yorick. Did you enjoy being a wit, a clown?"

"I did, Father. But I now know where God would have me serve."

I explained to him openly the reason for my banishment from Denmark, my disillusionment with court life in Scotland and England. I described how conversations with the Abbot at Winchelsea had persuaded me to change course, to revisit the calling I had rejected as a youth. When I had finished he remained silent in thought for some minutes. Then, "This is not a step to be lightly taken. Francis himself gave up a life of debauchery to serve the needy, but not without deep thought. Your own history as a fool makes me wonder whether you could truly abandon it for an ascetic existence with the Little Brothers. So I propose to put your resolve to the test."

"But ..."

"Let me finish. Two of the brotherhood leave here tomorrow for Ancona, whence they will sail North. Go with them to Venice. Find employment there as a jester. After that, if you are still determined to leave so cosseted a life behind we shall receive you back in Assisi, this time with a warmer welcome."

Chapter Thirteen
Iago

"There, where your argosies with portly sail –
Like signiors and rich burghers on the flood,
Or as it were, the pageants of the sea,
Do overpeer the petty traffickers."
[The Merchant of Venice, I, i]

The winds were propitious that wafted us to my reluctant destination. Venice, the great capital of commerce, basked in early morning sunlight as our craft breezed across the lagoon. A fleet of proud argosies, sails furled, lay off the shore. A flotilla of small boats, which I later learned were known as gondolas, plied busily to and fro carrying personnel and supplies for these ships, which were clearly preparing for their next voyage. As we approached the quayside I idly wondered about their destinations. Would they be heading westward to the ocean, then perhaps north to my distant homeland? Or were they bound for the Levant, to receive spices and silks from the orient? As it turned out, they would set sail that afternoon for a less remote island, though not all of them were destined to reach their goal. I was to discover this for myself all too soon. If only we had arrived at Venice a day later! But who am I to question God's mysterious ways?

As soon as we landed I asked my way to the Duke's palace, a sumptuous and elegant edifice overlooking the Piazza San Marco. What wealth and good taste was reflected in these gorgeous buildings! Elsinore was drab by comparison; the castles at Inverness and Dunsinane stark. I looked forward to my sojourn in this privileged place, as I delivered the letter of commendation I brought from Assisi. I was confident that my experience as a jester would secure me the employment Brother Ignatius wished me to taste before commiting myself to the Franciscan order. And so it did. But not as I expected.

The whole palace was abustle. Messengers hurried from chamber to chamber with such urgent demeanours that I hardly dared to intercept them, but in the end I managed to get directions to the Senators' bureau. The first Senator I encountered took a peremptory glance at my letter of introduction.

"Jester, eh?" he said with a dry laugh, "We could do with cheering up."

"Why, sir," I asked, "Is the city in mourning?"

"Soon will be, if the news is true. Damned Ottoman!"

"The Turk?"

"Who else? I only hope the task force will be in time."

"Task force, sir?"

"Still, if anyone can sort 'em out, the Moor will. And he'll be on his mettle for sure, to impress that pretty new wife of his. All the same, hell of a thing. Two hundred and thirty galleys, at the last count. Full of bloodthirsty

Turks with razor sharp scimitars. Wouldn't care to be in Cyprus when *they* get there." He paused for a moment as if visualising the scene of slaughter, then went on, "Jester, eh? Well, why not? Cheer them up when they arrive there. Might as well die laughing, what?" Again the humourless chuckle. "Report to Ensign Iago! Stout fella. Straight as the day is long. You'll find him organising the chandlers on the quayside. He'll fix you up with a ship."

"Thank you, sir!" I said without enthusiasm.

"Don't mention it. Good luck, whatever your name is!"

"It's Yor ..." but he'd gone, hotfooting it across the hall.

The Ensign to General Othello, the commander of the force being sent to relieve the garrison in Cyprus, was certainly straight-talking.

"Yorick?" He consulted his bills of lading, "No Yorick here. Who sent you?"

I explained that the unnamed Senator had referred me.

"No Yorick here," he frowned at me. "Foreigner, aren't you?"

"Danish."

"Not Turkey trash, are you? Not a spy?"

I showed him my letter of introduction.

"Clown, eh? Don't look too funny to me. Fat lot of use in a battle. Tell you what, the toffs will be able to use you. Get aboard that gondola there." He pointed at a craft that was just about to pull away. "That'll take you to the Duke of Milan's ship. She'll be dropping him off at Bari with the Prince of Naples. If you're lucky you'll stay with them instead of carrying on to Cyprus. Ain't going to be no picnic, when we get *there*."

I thanked him for the advice and made for the gondola. But before stepping aboard I was accosted by a tall cross-eyed fellow who was distinctly the worse for drink.

"And who might you be?" he asked.

"I've been sent to join Milan's vessel. I'm a jester."

"Name of Trinculo?"

"No, as a matter of fact. I'm ..."

"I thought not. Seeing as how I myself go by that dishtinguished nomencreature. You are an imposhter, sir!"

So saying, he fell into the gondola where he lay on his back and shouted "Take it away, Luigi!" The gondolier cast off and oared away towards the nearest argosy. I was left standing on the quayside. The brusque ensign saw me and sighed.

"OK, take the next one. You got money in your purse?" I shook my head. "Pot luck then, old son!"

Son? I was at least ten years his senior.

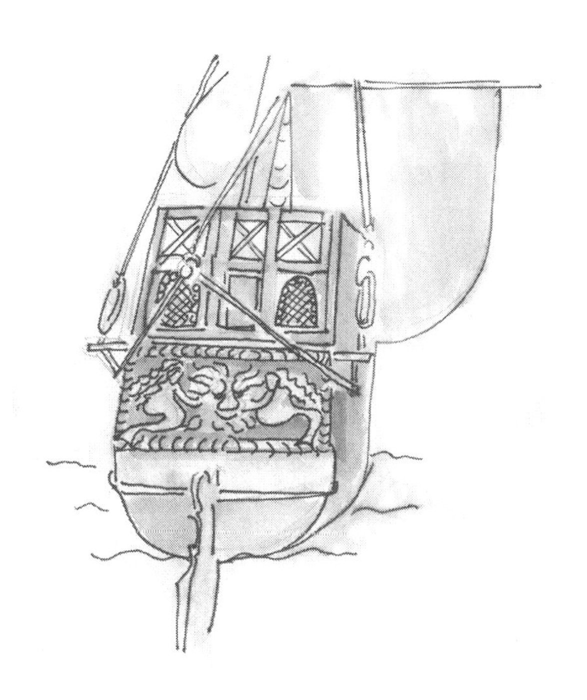

Chapter Fourteen

Illyria

"The wills above be done! But I would fain die a dry death."
[The Tempest, I, i]

I shared the next gondola to pull out across the lagoon with two young travellers, twins who hailed from Messaline. They were man and woman, though dressed as they were for the voyage, they were scarcely distinguishable. Before we reached our ship I learned that they had lost their mother when they were thirteen, their father sometime later. Why they were joining the expedition to Cyprus was a mystery. Perhaps he was seeking glory in the wars and she his twin could not bear to be separated from her brother. If so, before the next day dawned, their hopes were to be shattered.

The fleet set sail before nightfall. A freshening breeze meant that one after another the galleons traversed the narrow channel which took us to the open sea. Othello's stately flagship led the way, while our own vessel, abreast of that of the Duke of Milan, was soon left trailing. This was our misfortune. For as darkness fell the weather worsened and while most of the fleet sped southward without mishap, we were hit by what can be described only as a freak of a tempest. The wind intensified, whirling about us so that before the crew could fully reef the sails we were driven headlong towards the far coast. The last we saw of the Duke of Milan's poor argosy was when, illuminated by continual flashes of lightning, she keeled over on the rocky shore of some uncharted island. The storm had claimed its first wrecking and the lives of the fraughting souls within her.

But we had little time to pity them. Within the hour our own vessel had come to grief. The continuing gale hurtled us eastward. A light in the distance told us we were destined for an inhabited shore, but before we reached it our driving vessel struck a submerged bank. With a ghastly crack she split in two and all were flung into the raging waves. Those who found flotsam clung to it and swirled away in different directions. Other desperate souls, swimming and treading water, feared their briny ends had come. I was one of these forlorn castaways.

Although bereft of hope, I mouthed a heartfelt prayer for deliverance. And imagine my feelings when the wind dropped as suddenly as it had boiled up. What's more, the receding waves produced a further miracle. The bank on which our ship had foundered was but two or three feet below the surface. All the many survivors were able to stand with heads above the surface. The clouds having disappeared, we waded by moonlight through placid water towards the shore which we now realised was close at hand. Before long, our party gathered on the sandy beach which lay below a humble fishing village.

Sprawled on the sand recovering our breath, we rejoiced at our good fortune. All except one. It was the young woman I had accompanied aboard the gondola in Venice harbour. She was inconsolable. Her brother, her loving orphaned twin, had been swept away with the floating debris. Only the captain of our lost ship was able to give her any comfort. He claimed to have seen the youth attach himself to a strong mast which was swept away in the waves.

She dried her tears and fumbled at the purse which still hung from her soaking belt. As I recall, she said "For saying so, there's gold," then went on, "What country is this, my friend?"

"This, lady, is Illyria," he replied.

It seemed that the captain was a native of the place and as dawn broke he guided our raggle-taggle group through the nearby village and along the tracks which led to the main city of that Dukedom. Our clothes still being damp, we were grateful that the air was warm. Indeed, our spirits rose as did a friendly sun above the distant hills. From what the Captain told me of the Duke, a lover of music and the arts, it began to seem possible that I might find new employment as a jester in his court. My heart was still set upon priestliness, but I intended to test myself, as Ignatius in Assisi had insisted.

Illyria was a unique fiefdom. What its history was I never could discover, but I was astounded to find that the nobility (and their households) spoke only English although their names sounded Italian. There were two great families, which Orsino the Duke was attempting to bring together by marrying into the other. The object of his affection, the Lady Olivia, being in mourning for a dead brother, was resisting his overtures, filling him with an ostentatious melancholy. So much I learnt as we approached the city. This circumstance led me to doubt the possibility of either house welcoming a jester. However, after a day or two, when I had done what I could to make presentable my apparel, I approached Orsino's gatehouse.

Imagine my chagrin when I was pre-empted at the door by a long-faced fellow carrying a lute and clad in the garb of a jester! A guard greeted him like an old friend and ushered him into the palace. So I made my way to the hall of the Lady Olivia, arming myself with a plan to assuage her grief with some gentle wordplay and thus find favour and the employment I was becoming desperate to secure. An attendant at the gate sent for the steward, to whom I took an immediate dislike. Although a servant he bore a haughty demeanour, surveying me with visible distaste. His sober uniform marked him out as of severe outlook and no friend to jesting. Still, I explained my circumstances, throwing myself on his mercy.

"In this house of mourning there is no place for jests," he averred, "and if there were," (here he sniffed) "I would hardly pick one up from the gutter."

At this point we were both distracted by a burst of raucous laughter which emanated from within. The steward looked over his shoulder with a frown. Then, turning to me he said, "However, I do have need of a reliable underservant. Can you read?"

I assured him that I could command three or four

languages, word for word, without book.

"And might you, ahem, be ready to serve as my, how may I put it, eyes and ears? To keep me informed of any untoward below stairs behaviour?"

"Of course, sir," I said after some hesitation. Penniless, I was in no position to pick and choose.

"Very well. Your name?"

"Yorick."

"It's foreign-sounding."

"Danish. I'm from Denmark."

"Hm. Yor-rick. It won't do. Here you will be known as Fabian."

"Fabian? But why?"

He almost smiled. "Because last month I found it necessary to dismiss a servant woman when she was found to be with child. Most unfortunate, but one must maintain standards."

"But why Fabian?"

"What?"

"What has the poor woman's circumstance to do with my being labelled Fabian?"

"Ah, yes. Well, I like to have continuity."

I was baffled. "And?"

"Her name, you see, was Fabia. And mine is Malvolio. I am the Lady Olivia's steward. You, Fabian, will call me sir."

Not long after that I was to call him something less repeatable. Just as I was becoming accepted in the household and gaining the approval of the Lady Olivia, this Malvolio reported to her that I'd been seen at a bear-baiting. She, remaining in a somewhat excessive period of mourning, made her disappointment clear. I was relegated to attending her disreputable uncle Toby. This in turn led, in due course, to the renewal of my conviction that jesting was no longer for me. For the fooling to which I was party could only be described as excessively cruel.

Some might say that Malvolio deserved all that befell him; and that his fate was apt for an officious prig such as he. Yet I could not but pity him after his treatment by Feste, the clown I first encountered at Orsino's gate, who, having played on the steward's hopeless love for her Ladyship, had the fellow locked up like a lunatic and made the laughing stock of all the court. It left a bitter taste in the mouth after the joyful reunion of the Messalinean twins and their betrothals to the Duke and to the Lady Olivia. How callous of the jester then to sing heigh-ho the wind and the rain! I knew at that moment that I must follow my vocation into the caring profession of friar. I would return at once to Assisi.

Chapter Fifteen
Belmont

"This castle has a pleasant seat; the air
Nimbly and sweetly recommends itself
Unto our gentle senses."
[Macbeth, I, vi]

'At once' was more easily said than done. I could find no captain who was willing to take me south across the Adriatic Sea. Consequently forced to take to the tortuous coastal roads, I depended instead on the hospitality of strangers along the way. Sometimes I lodged in the humble homes of peasants who could ill afford the food they pressed on me. Other nights I passed in the company of well-padded monks, the richness of whose abbeys served to reinforce my conviction that, when in God's good time I became a friar, it should be with the frugal lifestyle of the Little Brothers of St Francis.

During the weary trek to Assisi one encounter stands out in my memory. Having trudged a whole long day across the plains of Venezia I came to a lofty castle named Belmont, where there was much ado that very day. Requesting shelter for the night I was welcomed at the gate with open arms and offered a hearty meal; but not without conditions. For the servants at that pleasant seat had been overwhelmed by important visitors, whose attendants and horses all required food and accommodation. Lords from Naples, France, England, Saxony, Morocco, Spain, Venice and even Scotland, had all been drawn to this place like bees to the hive. And the purpose of all this attention? To woo the daughter of the house, a lady whose beauty, I was told, matched her wisdom and understanding of the world. Moreover she was heiress to a huge fortune.

Portia's suitors were myriad. I was unsure whether they would have been so numerous had they seen her returning from her days in Venice, dressed in man's apparel. Evidently, she had been posing as a legal advocate in a case which threatened the life of an acquaintance. Having won the case, she was clearly happy to don her woman's weeds.

I spent several nights at Belmont, grateful to be well fed and to break the tedium of life on the road. But this was hardly a restful sojourn. In return for my keep I was expected to work in the stables, feeding, watering and cleaning up after the visitors' horses. And meanwhile the permanent staff of the castle kept me informed as to progress of the search for a husband for Portia. Her father had arranged a test which would identify a suitor with more sense than avarice and one by one the hopes of princes and lords were dashed until finally a Venetian nobleman took the prize.

This outcome was a huge relief to all the staff, who had feared that their new lord might have been one who spoke no Italian or, worse, a prince who would insist on their mistress being whisked off to live in Africa or the grim wastes of Scotland. It was also good to know that Belmont would no longer be besieged with suitors and their lackeys. As things calmed down, I availed myself of a day's rest before continuing my journey.

Chapter Sixteen

A Franciscan Fool

"Things have fall'n out, sir, so unluckily ..."
[Romeo and Juliet, III, iv]

Thus refreshed, and with the welcome aid of a ride on a tradesman's wagon, I soon reached the prosperous city of Padua, where marital plans of a different sort were being mooted. The talk of the place was that a rich gentleman named Baptista was having problems marrying off his eldest daughter. Her fiery temper had deterred all comers despite the promise of a healthy dowry. Whether or how the matter was resolved, I never did find out, for I wasted no time in heading south. But some years later I heard of a notorious court case in Pisa. A woman called

Katharina was tried for the murder of her husband. Defended by a young lawyer, Balthazar, she admitted to the killing and pleaded extreme provocation by the man. His servants gave evidence that he had indeed consistently behaved in an overbearing and arrogant manner and that the cooking pot she had thrown at him had first been hurled in the opposite direction. She was pardoned. It seemed possible to me that this was the same assertive woman I'd heard described in Padua.

Within days I reached Assisi and presented myself before Brother Ignatius. This time he was convinced of my calling and determination. I was enrolled as a novice of the order and began my long course of instruction in the devotional life of service with the Franciscan Order of the Little Brothers. Two years later, under my ordained name, I was dispatched to serve the people of Verona, where I was happy to counsel and shepherd the citizens for several years, until … But let my resumed journal tell the tragic tale.

The city is in turmoil. And no corner of the city is more riven with anguish than my chastened heart. Surely the call of Our Lord for me to serve him in the sombre grey of the Little Brothers was never meant to lead to such a melancholy disaster. I should have remained a jester. Then fate could never have played so black a joke.

Romeo and sweet Juliet are dead. Count Paris and the Lady Montague too! Two of the great Veronese houses, both alike in distress, are torn at the soul. And the cause? I, I am the cause. I, Friar Lawrence, the lovers' spiritual father, whose idiotic scheming has dragged them down to unshriven perdition. Alas the day!

Why did I encourage young Romeo in his passion? Had I not, then Juliet should have married the worthy Paris. As for Romeo, his nature was such that he should soon have fallen for another, Rosaline perhaps. After all, look at my case! I have now forgotten my dearest love, my Gertrude. Ah. Not completely forgotten, though she be lost to me and not even seen for fifteen years. Can it be so brief a time? My years in Britain; my treks through France and Lombardy; the adventure in Venice and Illyria; the course of meditation, study and prayer at the monastery; and my ministry here. Could all this have happened in so short a span? And that it should have come to so grievous an outcome! May God forgive me and guide me to the means of atonement.

I imagined that I had left all chaos behind me when I abandoned the persona of Yorick, to be rechristened Lawrence by the Holy Father. I even wrote, in the guise of a fictitious cleric, a letter to my beloved Queen Gertrude back in Denmark (lives she still?). I told her Yorick was dead, which in a sense was true. That long chapter of my life was at an end.

The new episode then began. I became the humble friar, sworn to poverty and service, to live out my final years ministering to the people of Verona. I would nurture not only their spiritual health but also, using my skills with nature's medicaments, their bodily well-being. For by now I found myself exceptionally adept at creating and applying the many restorative potions to be had from plants and minerals. All beneficent! Not from me would sufferers ever obtain the poisons peddled by certain unscrupulous apothecaries.

Alas, how could I have guessed that banished Romeo in his desperation would go to one such mountebank? What diabolical intervention stopped the good Friar John from delivering to the youth my letter, which would have averted disaster? Cruel was the fate that took Romeo to the dead-seeming Juliet before she awoke from the sleep my distillation had induced. It is as if a perverse Will were at work, moulding events to create some tragic drama.

Yet I am to blame. My dream, to reconcile the proud and feuding Capulets and Montagues, was doomed to end in nightmare. I should have foreseen it. And now, what irony! Those august houses are indeed united. United in grief.

Immured in my spartan cell, I await the Prince's verdict on my unintended crime. After the discovery of the bodies he declared that he had always recognised me as a holy man but I know that in the interests of the city he cannot ignore this tragic circumstance. I hope that he will choose to banish me. I shall then seek ways to atone for my errors. Exile would be my excuse to flee Verona, where I shall ever be known as the fool who caused the deaths of Romeo and Juliet.

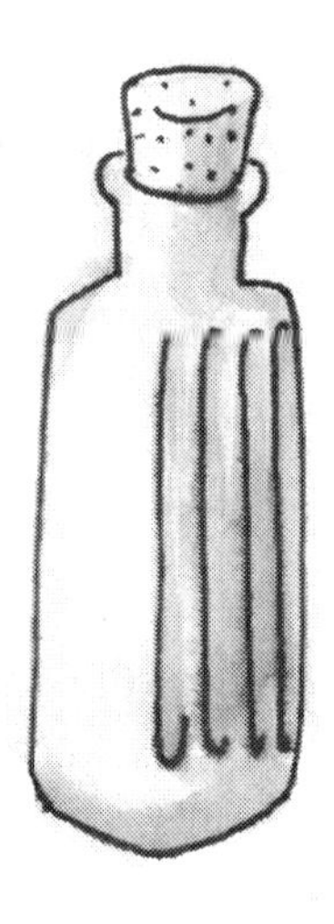

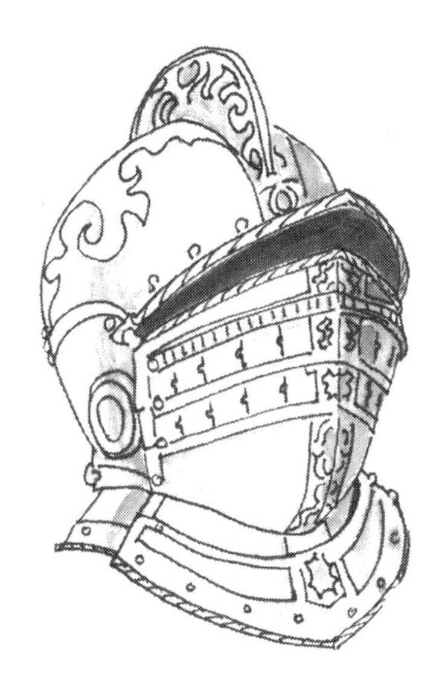

Chapter Seventeen

Milan

"... for Friar Laurence met them both,
As he in penance wander'd through the forest."
[Two Gentlemen of Verona, V, ii]

And so it came to pass. I was banished from Verona and made my way to the great city of Milan, there to commence my programme of atonement. My intention was to keep away from the world of power and wealth, where so much of my life had been spent. I had no appetite to return to the service of kings and aristocrats. I longed to embrace the simplicity and innocence to which St Francis came after the sinful looseness of his younger days. So, having registered with the Duke my presence in his territory, I attempted to adopt a Sabine existence of isolation and self-denial. It was not to last. My journal explains why.

I was astounded. I resolved to go at once to the Duke, even though the Palace, indeed the whole of the city of Milan, makes too busy a setting for my planned year of solitary penitence. It was his daughter Silvia. I could not believe it.

But it certainly was she. The woman was masked, so that I could possibly have been mistaken, but no! Her very walk was Silvia's and her voice too when she greeted me with a dignified "Good evening". I was not wrong. Nor was the good Friar Patrick when he had overheard Sir Eglamour outside the abbey wall. Let me recall, he heard the knight muttering to himself that Silvia would not fail to meet him, "for lovers break not hours unless it be to come before their time". Those were his very words. And then a young woman's footsteps.

Soon after that, my lonely prayers for Heaven's pardon after my errors in Verona were disturbed by the couple's hurried tread on the trail through the forest.

Sir Eglamour! Who would have believed it? An honourable knight of mature years who, after the death of his dear wife and one true love, vowed lifelong celibacy. And there he was, arm in arm with a young woman; no less than the daughter of the Duke of Milan. I accosted them at once. Memories of last year flooded my mind. The parallel with Juliet's fateful elopement was too close for the comfort of my soul. I knew that I had to discourage these ill-matched lovers.

"Good Eglamour," I said. This was no time for niceties, "In God's name be advised by me! Return to the city, where I shall be your advocate for the Duke's clemency, should it become known that you have been so rash."

At this he paled and appeared nervous which I took to be

a prudent wavering in his resolve to ruin the lady. But before I could press my case she seized his arm and swept him off in the direction of Mantua, exclaiming "Come away!" And calling back over her shoulder, "Fear not, old friar! His intentions are of the purest." They were gone.

"Old friar, indeed!" I am scarce fifty-one.

As for Sir Eglamour's intentions, whatever they may be, they cannot please the Duke who has his own plans for Silvia's choice of husband. Already he has rejected the advances of two eligible gentlemen of Verona. Besides, the forest is notoriously the haunt of outlaws. I must waste no further time in reporting my discovery to the Duke.

Chapter Eighteen

Two Brother Dukes

*"They live like the old Robin Hood of England ...
And fleet the time carelessly, as they did in
the golden world."*
[As You Like It, I, i]

Praise God! I have faced a devil and by The Lord's good grace have brought his soul to salvation. Yet what terror was mine before the Holy Spirit prevailed! How close to torture and a violent death I came! Now at last I believe that I was right to take up Holy Orders and leave behind my life of jesting.

It all happened in the Forest of Arden, or Ardenne as some would have it. What you will. My year of penance being complete, I had decided to make the long trek from Milan to the land of my birth. This was despite having learnt that Denmark was still ruled by King Hamlet and his Queen. There was little risk now that my grey beard, bald pate, stout form and careworn visage might be recognised as the nimble Yorick who twenty years before had sung, joked and tumbled his jolly trade at Elsinore. Besides, the Holy Father in Rome had sent out word that mendicants fluent in the Danish tongue were greatly needed there.

The Duke of Milan, in gratitude for my small part in the happy match made between his daughter Silvia and the worthy Valentine, aided my journey by authorising a document to ease my passage through the more unruly states. Thus I travelled in safety through Savoy to Burgundy and then Northward. I traversed Champagne, indebted to peasants, priors and charitable householders for their hospitality. And reached the wild woods of Arden. Reputedly, the region is infested with brigands, yet I met with only kindness from the local shepherds and groups of gentlefolk who, shunning the sophistication of courtly life, had chosen to live in sylvan simplicity under the greenwood tree.

What a shock awaited me after I left them and proceeded through the northern skirts of the forest! Rounding a bend in the track, I was confronted by a troop of armed horsemen.

I was seized, bound, gagged and unceremoniously thrown across the haunches of a mule. Thence they bore me away in triumph, for all the world as if they had captured the warlike caliph of Aleppo.

At their encampment, which bristled with soldiery, I was bundled along to the most sumptuous of the tents and dumped at its guarded entrance. There I lay bewildered. After what seemed hours I was pulled to my feet and dragged inside. My gag was removed. I looked up into the baleful eyes of a boarlike aristocrat, his throne flanked by a pair of ferocious pikeholders.

"Name?" demanded the graceless fellow.

Before I could reply I was struck the most painful blow between the shoulder-blades. It would have pitched me to the floor had I not been pinioned by two muscular guards.

"Name!!" he repeated.

"My name is Lawrence, sir and, as you may judge by my habit, I travel this way to do the work of the Lord."

"Oh yes? By whose say so?"

"By the example of Our Lord Jesus Christ and his beloved Saint Francis."

"Indeed? And was it them who told you to trespass on my domain?" With this he nodded to one of the guards and I suffered another vicious punch. It took me a minute to recover my breath.

"Answer the High Duke Frederick!" hissed my other captor, digging his nails into my elbow. In my mind I uttered a prayer that I might be delivered from this evil company and given strength to bear the pain.

"Your honour," I said, "I have in my time served great kings and princes, whom I have had the privilege to amaze and mystify, as well as ministering to their spiritual hunger…"

"Tchah!" the Duke retorted, "I want information, not

ministration. Tell me what I need to know and you'll go free. Otherwise …" His gesture conveyed the summary slitting of my throat.

"What do you seek?"

"My brother. One who, I am informed, is gathering about him in the forest a force to usurp my Dukedom. An army of outlaws and ne'er-do-wells!"

I took a moment to gather my thoughts then responded, "Sir, I have heard of younger brothers among the nobility who in jealousy have plotted to wrest away the birthright of the eldest son. Such acts are damnable in God's eyes. Such sinners are doomed to hellfire and eternal torment."

Instead of agreeing, the Duke appeared taken aback. I went on, "If therefore I am able to do anything, anything at all, to rescue your brother's soul from everlasting perdition it is my Christian duty – and yours too, sir, – to do so."

Duke Frederick took time to digest this thought, so I continued, "Describe your brother! I observed no warlike preparations during my passage through the forest other than your own horsemen. However, I may unwittingly have heard some pertinent information." He remained silent, staring at me in bemusement, until I added "Is he your junior by many years?"

The Duke of a sudden addressed his guards. "Let him loose!" My arms were released, which was a mercy. To me he said "Please sit down." The guards looked puzzled but hurried forward with a stool, which I was grateful to accept. Meanwhile, he stood up and began pacing to and fro. He dismissed his men. When we were alone he turned to face me with an earnest frown.

"You spoke of hellfire?"

"I did. He who defies the divine right of inheritance is

damned. There shall be weeping and gnashing of teeth. Your brother's soul is in grave danger, sire."

The man sat again. He seemed visibly shrunk, a crumpled version of the proud bully who had launched my interrogation. When he finally spoke, his voice was laden with emotion, barely audible. "That dread prospect is not my brother's, father. He *is the senior. I am the usurper. What shall I do to be saved?"*

The ensuing weeks we spent together in prayer and questioning, in meditation and discourse. Before a month had passed Frederick had assigned his curtilege back to the brother from whom he had seized the Dukedom by force. He undertook solemn vows of commitment to the religious life of the true penitent. I am sure there was joy in Heaven. There was certainly joy in the Forest of Arden when the Duke Senior received news of his peaceful restoration. On his return he greeted his convertite brother with a tearful embrace of forgiveness.

Tomorrow I shall continue my journey with a new assurance that my calling to the Cloth was no delusion. I have helped to quash an unjust war. I have rescued the tarnished soul of the false Duke. I have restored his gentle brother to his rightful heritage and title. I shall now return to Denmark with fresh belief that I may find worthwhile work in the service of God and my Homeland.

Chapter Nineteen

Wittenberg

"... the players ... are the abstracts and brief chronicles of the time: ..."
[Hamlet, II, ii]

My way now lay towards Saxony, where I was to meet up with an old friend. The visit led to an extraordinary encounter. I recorded it before leaving the city.

Nothing could have prepared me for the maelstrom of pride and satisfaction, yet tinged with regret, which awaited me when I broke my journey to visit Friar Ludwig. A reverend colleague at Assisi and my closest friend during my time there, Ludwig is now teaching divinity at the university in Wittenberg.

This afternoon, the third and last of my stay here, I was given a tour of this venerable seat of learning. I was impressed by the several libraries and lecture halls. I spent some time in prayer before the famous altarpiece by one Cranach, a former Burgomeister of the town. However, I declined to enter the doors of All Saints' Church, defiled as they have been by the erroneous 'Articles' nailed there in recent times by Herr Luther. Yet I hasten to add that my current turmoil of mind is unconnected with the schism that gentleman seeks to incite. I have no doubt that it will come to nothing and in a year or two the name Martin Luther will be forgotten.

What has stirred me so deeply is an event that came later in the day. The evening began ordinarily enough, when I was taken to dine at one of the town's coaching inns. Ludwig and I were intrigued to find the courtyard occupied by preparations for a performance of some kind. It emerged that a troupe of travelling players had arrived. They were to present a tragedy entitled 'The Murder of Gonzago'. Already the tiers about the yard were filling up with excited students. Within me, some latent desire to touch my past as an entertainer caused me to request that we stay to watch the play. Ludwig was happy to agree.

As we took our places, leaning over an upper balcony, I noticed a buzz of activity among the student groundlings. One of the players, already costumed and bearded, was squatting at the edge of the platform in conversation with a particular group. Eventually, one young man raised a hand. His companions let out a delighted cheer as this volunteer was lifted onto the stage and led away by the actor. He was a tall fellow with ginger hair, who winked at his friends as he disappeared behind the scenery.

Before the tragedy began, the bearded player stepped forward to announce there'd been a casualty among the cast.

This news invoked good-humoured groans and boos from the groundlings in the pit. However, the thespian went on, a local actor had been found to deputise. This was greeted with cheers and applause. The speaker bowed low and withdrew.

At once the action commenced. I saw that our red-haired friend was now royally robed and crowned. He proceeded across the stage with a convincingly regal gait, arm in arm with his consort. It soon became clear that this queen was whispering the new recruit through a dumb depiction of the whole plot. Even so, the audience, which might have been expected to make fun of one of their own number, watched in rapt silence.

Once the story had been completed in mime, including the ghastly poisoning of the King by his brother, the play proper was performed in rhyming couplets. This time the stand-in sat, stood or moved while projecting the mood of the words as they were declaimed by an actor concealed behind drapes. Again, the watchers were engrossed, such was the stage presence of this understudy. The groundlings gave voice only when the murderer, a caricatured villain, entered to a chorus of hissing and catcalls.

At the end there erupted a wave of applause. No performer received a louder cheer than our ginger-headed student. I leant towards a stranger at my side to ask, "Who is this student-king? He has a future as an actor."

"Sadly, not as a professional," came the reply, "He studies philosophy at the university but soon goes home to Denmark. His name is Hamlet."

I was stunned, dizzy with surprise. It was my son! For a moment I had to hold onto the balustrade. Friar Ludwig frowned in concern.

"Are you unwell, Lawrence?"

I recovered my composure. "Quite the reverse!" In truth I

was ecstatic. "I should like to congratulate that young fellow in person. Most exhilarating!"

Ludwig was surprised that I should over-enthuse regarding a play which after all was a naive and unexceptional piece. Nevertheless he agreed and led me down a staircase to where the groundlings were still milling about.

All at once I was face to face with Hamlet. I shook him warmly by the hand, careful not to betray the surge of fatherly love with which my heart was brimming. He accepted my congratulations with a careless grace before moving on to speak to a colleague. I overheard this fellow say, "There are more talents in you, Hamlet, than you could dream of in your Philosophy." Then they swept off into the tavern.

And now, back in the modest cell which is my resting place this night, I am flooded with emotions. With joy, that I have seen and spoken with my secret son. With pride, that he should be so accomplished in holding an audience, an ability which I myself achieved only after years of application. And with regret, such deep regret, that I have missed all the years which brought him from infancy to noble manhood. The King and Gertrude have raised him well.

Chapter Twenty

Return to Elsinore

"Never excuse; for when the players are all dead, there need none to be blamed."
[A Midsummer-Night's Dream, V, i]

My Franciscan grey bought me safe passage northward for the following week, until I reached the harbour at Rostock. There I met a messenger from the royal court at Elsinore who was himself commissioning a vessel to take him there. I joined him and three days later was on the quayside in my home city. Little had changed. The great castle loomed over the grey houses huddled round its walls. And it was raining, just as I remembered it. I followed the King's emissary up the hill and presented my Church credentials to the Prime Minister's Secretary.

"The Lord Polonius will like this," he commented, "The old Chaplain is on his last legs. You speak Danish?"

I assured him it was my native tongue.

"Wait here, then!"

I stood beneath the portal peering into the Lower Ward and across to the chapel which I had known so well. I wondered whether the 'old chaplain' could be my mentor Father Gregory, but realised this was impossible. Many years had passed since my banishment.

And then I saw her. The Queen. My Gertrude, as elegant as ever, attended by a pair of ladies-in-waiting. She hurried from one archway to another and disappeared into the Great Hall. My heart raced with the excitement of seeing her; then sank as I remembered that she would never recognise me, indeed would believe me dead, assuming she had ever received my letter from Verona.

The Secretary returned. He gave me a nod of approval and led me to the simple chamber that was to be my home for the next ten years. Here I ministered to the needs, spiritual and apothecarial, of the Royal Household. Here I could feel close to those I had once loved above all others – the old King Hamlet, the Prince (my unmentionable son!) and the Queen. It was the longest and most settled period of my life. And it ended in a manner unpredictable, although nothing could be certain as long as Claudius lived close by.

To tell you what in the end befell requires a cleverer hand than mine. Therefore I turn to my talented friend Osric. He once heard Prince Hamlet describe him as a 'waterfly' but I know him to be quite brilliant in his own way, witty and perceptive and moreover a bard in his own right. I can do no better than to reproduce a drama he wrote. It describes what happened at Elsinore one fateful day as well as the circumstances which made those events possible.

Here it follows. Osric may have poetised the words that were used, but their meaning tells a true account of what he witnessed and recorded. If you can imagine that all that had gone before could be presented as a five-act play, then this might be entitled …

Hamlet Act Six

Dramatis Personae

FORTINBRAS: Prince of Norway
HAMLET: Prince of Denmark
POLONIUS: Lord Chamberlain
LAERTES: Son of Polonius
OLD HAMLET: King of Denmark
CLAUDIUS: King of Denmark
AN OLD PRIEST
Two clowns, Gravediggers
GERTRUDE: Queen of Denmark and Mother to Hamlet
OPHELIA: Daughter to Polonius

Scene: Elsinore, a Hall in the Castle

(Draped about two thrones are the bodies of Gertrude and – his crown askew – Claudius. The corpses of Hamlet and Laertes lie below. Young Fortinbras is addressing troops and onlookers who are offstage.)

FORTINBRAS. … so have we heard
Of carnal, bloody and unnatural acts,
Of accidental judgements, casual slaughters,

Of deaths put on by cunning and forced cause,
And, in this upshot, purposes mistook
Fall'n on the inventors' heads.
For me, with sorrow I embrace my fortune.
I have some rights of memory in this kingdom,
Which now to claim my vantage doth invite me
Don this crown.

(Taking the crown from Claudius' head, putting it on)

Let four captains
Bear Hamlet like a soldier to the stage;
For he was likely, had he been put on,
To have proved most royally.

(A commotion. Enter Priest)

PRIEST. And shall so still! I seize this coronet!

(Lifting crown from Fortinbras)

FORTINBRAS. Impudent cleric! Thou deluded man,
Yield up that royal emblem of the state
Unto thy rightful liege, on pain of death!

PRIEST. Yet hear me first, Prince Fortinbras! And when
My wondrous tale thou hast accoustered,
Take this from this if thou acknowledge not
That my rash seizure of the Danish crown
Be justful, by the holy law of kings.

FORTINBRAS. We shall give audience, reckless priest. Yet know
The wolves of justice shall descend on thee,

Should truth prove contra in conviction.

PRIEST. So, kin of mighty Norway, let it be.
But first I'd quiz thee. Who, and answer true,
On Claudius' decease should take the throne?

FORTINBRAS. Why, Hamlet, son of Denmark's warrior lord
That slew my own great father in the wars.
He who himself measures the ground in death.

PRIEST. And Hamlet is alive.

FORTINBRAS. Tush, foolish friar!
Unbreathing lies his melancholy corse
And cold his noble blood has ceased its flow,
Yielding to mortal wound.

PRIEST. Yet look again!

FORTINBRAS. What alchemy is here? The body breathes.
There's crimson in his lips. Now flush his cheeks.
He lives!

PRIEST. Be not afrighted, sir!

FORTINBRAS. Satan's thy god,
That can bestir the very dead.
Angels and ministers of grace defend us!

PRIEST. Soft, sir! No devil's work is here at play,
But God's involvement solely. Hamlet's cut
Was slighter than the briar's petty scratch
When thorough the woods the huntsman heedless strides

To close his prey. Him poison overcame.

FORTINBRAS. Poison?

PRIEST. Upon Laertes treacherous foil!
This know I, for the source of that fell juice
Stands here before you. Thus saved I the life
Of Denmark's Prince.

FORTINBRAS. With poison saved his life? How say you so?

PRIEST. Sir, though a Dane, I long in Italy dwelt,
Where, tutored by a holy hermit sage
I came to con the virtues excellent
Of baleful weeds and precious-juiced flowers.
Oh, muckle is the powerful grace that lies
In plants, herbs, stones and their true qualities.
Now mark! When young Laertes first did hear
Of's father's end, and at Prince Hamlet's hand,
He came to me with tale of anguish'd dog,
Distempered unto pain but not to death.
Quoth he, this hound I love I would dispatch,
As life for him is naught but agony.
With direst warnings of its dread effects –
To beast, or man, delivering certain doom –
I served his wishes with a tincture …

FORTINBRAS. Venomous?

PRIEST. Aye, fatal in its superficial signs!
In essence, though, an unction innocent,
Yielding but loan'd resemblance of decease.

In brief, you witness here a butterfly death,
Now lit, now flown, until the destin'd day
When good Prince Hamlet's soul should heavenward soar.
See, he awakes.

FORTINBRAS. And with his waking, lo!
My reign in Denmark thus is ended so.
Norwegians, Come!

(Exit Fortinbras. Hamlet stirs)

HAMLET. The rest is silence.

PRIEST (aside) Now my stratagem,
I thank thee God, comes to fruition.
And in bleak Denmark my atonement
For cruel miscarriage in Italian climes
Enabled is. Hamlet! My lord! Awake!

HAMLET. O wondrous! I methought was ta'en to heaven,
And flights of angels sang me to my rest.
But soft, what fiend on yonder throne holds sway
Over our sovereign land in drunken snore?
Usurper of my kindly father's life,
My mother's virtue and my country's crown!
Here's sword. Now might I do it pat. Yet wait!
Tricks o' the mind delude me. Certain sure,
Ere that fond dream that I had flown above,
I slew my devil uncle doubly o'er
With poison – on the blade, and i' the wine

Which heinous Claudius prepared for me
And was my mother's bane. Yet one, two, three
A catchy sequence is. I top him thrice.
This bodkin bare shall serve.

PRIEST. Hold! Stay thy hand!
Thine uncle lifeless lies.

HAMLET. Good holy man,
Who my confessor's been these half-score years,
Purge me of all these murky murderous thoughts!
Pronounce me worthy of my country's throne
Which I perceive, from this most bloody wreck,
And the sad passing of my dam and queen
Becomes my seat of governance, by right.

(Reaches out to take crown from priest)

PRIEST. Contrition well becomes thee, goodly prince.
Yet must accession to the rule of Danes
Keep thee awaiting for a later time.
Behold thy mother!

(Gertrude stirs, sighs. Hamlet goes to her)

HAMLET. That fell sergeant, Death,
Though strict in his arrest, releaseth thee.
Dear mother!

GERTRUDE. Son! What phantasy was here!
I dreamt that poison stole away my breath
Ending the turmoil of my harrow'd life.

Mine eyes once more beheld the wholesome form
Of thy great father's person, worthy king.
Alas, with recall to this realm of care
I ope my eyes to find foul Claudius there.

HAMLET. Lov'd queen and mother, sure my father's soul
Has wing'd its flight to God's celestial haven,
Yet comfort thee with this. Yon tyrant cur
My uncle, fuell'd by's crimes commit on Earth
Now fryeth in the very flames of Hell.
He's dead indeed. And thou this crown shalt wear.

(Places crown on her brow)

GERTRUDE. Good friar, a word!
Methinks that in the corner of thine eye
There gleams some knowledge of these strange behaps.
I charge thee, by the majesty of state,
Recount the means by which they came to pass.

PRIEST. Madame, I shall. When first I fled these shores
In banishment for sin of treasonous hue,
Afar I journeyed; gambols, songs and mirth,
My life before, leaving in Denmark. Then
In holy orders consolation found,
And with it wisdom of the natural world.
As saintly Francis conversed with the beasts,
So I from plants did garner harvest rich
Of medicines and distillations rare.
Until one woeful hap, which I do weep

To think upon and cannot cease to do.
Chastened, to Denmark I returned, grey hairs
And habit drear concealing what I'd been,
Yea, e'en from those whose hearts had once been mine.

HAMLET. Come to't, old priest!

(Laertes yawns, listens)

PRIEST. Claudius the King,
Or rather, as then he was, mean sibling
To's royal brother Hamlet, knowing of
My skill in Medication, sought of me
A draught of hebona, an essence fell
In function and most merciless to life.
With protest did I yield to his command
Except in this. The potion he received
From me was but my counterfeited dram,
Whose work would mimic death, for a brief span.

GERTRUDE. Ah! This was then the tincture in the cup
That stole Prince Hamlet's breath a while, and mine!

(Laertes leaps up, sword in hand)

LAERTES. And mine! Curst Hamlet, meet thy doom!

PRIEST. Laertes, now beseech you, sweet thy words
With honey of calm and reconcilement!

LAERTES. I'll not be juggled with. Yon vilesome
prince

Did slay my father, whose white locks deserved
Not murder but the reverence of old age.
And my dear sister, fair Ophelia, plunged
To her dank grave in madness, driv'n by him.

HAMLET. I loved Ophelia!

LAERTES. Damned Hamlet, die!

PRIEST. Halt! Stay thy hand, Laertes! Thou shalt see
Justice for all the ills thy house has borne.
Come forth!

(Enter Polonius)

GERTRUDE. Polonius! What, art thou a ghost?
Now do I dream again, or spirits walk.

LAERTES. O vision of my fallen father, speak!

POLONIUS. Laertes. Son. My blessing on thee, thus!
I see that thou my precept hast forgot.
Look thou remember, give thy thoughts no tongue,
Nor any unproportion'd thought his act,
Til thou ...

LAERTES. Father, 'tis thee, 'tis sure. Embrace
Thy son in love!

GERTRUDE. Polonius lives? But how?

PRIEST. When summoned to the court,

Last rites to min'ster to his parting soul,
I sensed a tiny sliver still of life
In his pierced trunk – a spirit loth to die!
With precious herbs and juice of obscure flower
I nurtured that dim spark of life to flame,
Then to the blaze of being that here you see.

HAMLET. Polonius, I kneel before you thus
To supplicate for thy forgiveness.
I struck at thee mistaking for a rat
Named Claudius. Your pardon, worthy sir!
And yours, Laertes! May this happy stance
Placate what else should be a righteous rage,
Befitting vengeance dire.

LAERTES. To Hell with that!
No ministering monk was there to clutch
From the dread maw of death that angel pure,
Sweet maid, dear sister, kind Ophelia.
Thou, reverend, shouldst tremble, sigh and weep
For impotence to save her precious life.
I to myself would prove myself untrue
Should I withhold to vengeance take – on you!

(Launching himself at Hamlet)

POLONIUS. Laertes! Son! I charge thee, rant no more!
Feast thou thine eyes instead on yonder door!

(Enter Ophelia)

Wonder indeed! Aye, view her in amaze!

LAERTES. Ophelia! Angel sister! This day's joys
March in procession wondrous. Father, tell,
How comes this joyous miracle to pass?

POLONIUS. Child. I may call thee so, though man thou art,
Yet wert thou once a child, and child of mine.
But let that pass. What thinkst thou of me now?

LAERTES. Why, as my sage and honourable sire,
Etched with the dignity of passing years.

POLONIUS. Dear boy, I fain would prove so. What then shouldst
Thou've done but gape, had you been there to watch?
I say to watch, yet with thy sportive frame
Thou surely would have overcapp'd my deed,
Thyself to save th'imperill'd life of sweet
Ophelia. Yet be that as it may …
Where was I?

OPHELIA. Here take I up the baton. And in truth
Would sprint to Sparta stern from Marathon
In words, so pent up is my urge to tell
The world beyond the close that's been my home
These weeks, since dear my father showed his age
To be illusion. First must I plead
With each of you, for pardon. I have sinn'd
And worked deception on you all. For in
Despair that ever I might gain the man
Whose conquest was and is the only goal
Of my heart's passion, I did cruelly ape

Distraction. The madness that I feigned
Was but to conjure pity in the heart
Of my heart's heart. Yet ere I could return
To him, to reinforce my earnest plea,
Ill-fitting though such importuning were
For daughter of a courtly noble grave –
Forgive me, father – Death play'd dice with me.
Well named is the die we throw when match'd
With that grim keeper of the ultimate bourne.
For, gath'ring pendant garlands from the trees,
I overreach'd myself, and headlong fell
Into the thirsty brook, which drank me down
To silty depth of blackness.

PRIEST. By God's grace
It happened in the self-same blink of time
That in the dusk we stroll'd, as was our wont
Along the bosky virons of a stream,
Close to the cell wherein we spent our days –
I mean myself and good Polonius.
That lord, now full recovered from the wound
Inflicted by th'o'erhasty Prince's thrust,
Reluctant yet to show himself in court,
Sore with prick'd pride that the funereal rites
Accorded to the corse believed to be
That of Polonius, Denmark's premier,
Should be dismiss'd with hugger-mugger haste
By the decree of Claudius.

LAERTES. So I learn'd
Too late to amend, ere I from Paris came.

POLONIUS. Allow me to conclude this rambling tale!
'Rambling' indeed, as we did 'ramble' there,
Deep in converse of sage divinity.
Our words were interrupted by a sound
Of gasp and splash and floundering of limbs.
Beheld we then the vision of a nymph
E'en in the act of sinking out of sight.
What mysteries encompass humankind!
Where flew my stiffness, whither fled my years,
When, on the instant, to the depths I dove,
I sought, I clasp'd, I dredged my daughter out?
And Jove be praised, my darling was alive,
Conscious, until she gazed into the face
Of her suppos'd dead father. Whereat she
Askance, did faint away with sigh profound.

LAERTES. O wondrous! Then have I a sister yet.
But soft! How can such circumstance prevail?
This Prince and I did wrestle o'er thy grave
In disrespectful brawl.

PRIEST. Oh, wonder not!

HAMLET. Thy medicine?

(Claudius is recovering)
PRIEST. Indeed, for while the departing herd
Of grieving courtiers wound across the lea,
We bore Ophelia to a caring nurse,
Whose dumb devotion has her health restor'd.

OPHELIA. Since when the goodly friar did anchor us

Within the haven of his hermit's cell
Until the winds blew fair to waft us back
Safely to court.

CLAUDIUS. A touching tale! My Queen, I'll have the crown.

(He dons the crown, takes the throne)

Wherefore this crop of reconcilement sweet
Hath sprouted from the soil of gory deeds
I know not, nor I care.

POLONIUS. In brief, my lord ...

CLAUDIUS. In brief is not thy forte. What is done
Is done. Come Gertrude, sit you at my side!
The tiller of the ship of Denmark's state
Demands a steady hand, and that is mine.

HAMLET. Fell villain! Vilest prince
That ever throne defiled! Now steal I leave
To pledge just loyalty to the land of Danes.
Blest realm of heroes bred in Northern Climes
To thrive amidst adversity and war!
Denmark, poor Denmark, thou hast suffered dear
Beneath the cruel heel of this false king,
Who is the rotten something in the state
Oft spoke of in the annals of our times.
Now vow I here beneath the arched roofs
Of weary Elsinore, where once did rule
The greatest of the monarchs of the North,

I mean my father, rest his blessed soul,
I promise …

VOICE OFF (Old Hamlet). Swear!

HAMLET. I here do vow to …

VOICE OFF. Swear!

HAMLET. Art yet about? Poor ghost, I'll follow thee.

(Exit Hamlet. A hullabaloo)

GERTRUDE. Hamlet, my son!

(Exit Gertrude in pursuit)

PRIEST. Come, friends, we'll to his aid.
Who knows what demons haunt the misty towers
And battlements, to fling him to his doom!

(Exeunt Friar, Laertes with drawn sword, Polonius and Ophelia)

CLAUDIUS. So, Hamlet, 'scaped from death by poison'd blade,
May soon discover thy end's by puncture made.

(Exit Claudius, drawing a dagger)
(Enter Laertes, sheathing his sword)

LAERTES. I'll let them press the search.

How quick does disillusion chill the soul!
The mightiest oak that o'er the forest rules
May still at heart a gnawing fungus feed,
Consuming in its monumental trunk
The very substance of its strength immense.
Better by far that puny man should reap
Its giant timbers for the struts and keel
Of galleon or sturdy man-of-war
To grace the oceans, than that its mossied height
Should measure on the shadowed ground its fall
From grandeur to the habitat demean
Of termite, snail and scuttling cockroach vile.
So might my fate befall in Denmark here.
Thanks to the machinations of yon priest
I live, but all the former righteous ire
Which fused the cannon of my vengeful rage
And sped me back from France, is now discharg'd
In meaningless and empty bombast.
Avenge my father's murder? Yet he lives.
Kill Hamlet for he drove my sister mad?
It was her subterfuge and, as her death,
Delusion. I'll back to Paris, me.
My doddering, preaching father; and Ophelia,
Who'd feign a lunacy to get her wish,
I'll leave behind in Denmark. Tis the day
When from youth's apron-strings I'll break away!

(Exit Laertes. Knocking within)

FIRST CLOWN (off). Coo-ee! Coo-ee!

SECOND CLOWN (off). Coo-ee! Coo-ee!

(Knocking within. Enter two clowns, a sexton and mate)

FIRST CLOWN. Listen to it, Knock, knock, knock!

SECOND CLOWN. Knock, knock, knock!

FIRST CLOWN. Knock, knock? There's no knocking I know of that can raise the dead.

SECOND CLOWN. Faith, there is too.

FIRST CLOWN. How say you so?

SECOND CLOWN. Why, the knocking on the coffins at Doomsday, when all the dead of the ages shall be woken up and walk around.

FIRST CLOWN. Thou says well, good master gravedigger. But thou shalt see no human knockers that could bring a man to stand again.

(Pause. Second Clown points to a woman in the audience)

I stand corrected. But to our task!
(Wordlessly sings the Dead March)

SECOND CLOWN. Be that our task?

FIRST CLOWN. Why, verily! Join thou along!

(They sing together)

SECOND CLOWN. How is this? Were we not sent to the castle here to measure the dead, that the graves should befit the royal corpses? Twere pity should we fail in so solemn a measurement!

FIRST CLOWN. Why what is this air but a solemn measure indeed!

(Both fall about laughing. More singing)

SECOND CLOWN. Nay, 'tis but a grave tune!

(More hilarity - this time only from Second Clown)

FIRST CLOWN. But soft, where be the royal remains? Where the King?

SECOND CLOWN. Where the Queen?

FIRST CLOWN. And the Prince Hamlet?

SECOND CLOWN. Where the young Laertes? *(To man in audience).* What have you done, milord, with the dead bodies?
FIRST CLOWN. Nay, now! Be there no corpses, then I can guess the purpose for our being here. 'Tis nowt but comic relief.

SECOND CLOWN. Twas the interlude! Here comes Prince Hamlet, as alive as you like. Come, let's seek out a stoup of liquor!

(Exeunt clowns. Enter Hamlet)

HAMLET. My father's phantom doth elude me still
Yet baleful Claudius lives and reigns, while I,
The very incarnation of self doubt
In hesitancy hover at the gate
Of action resolute, ne'er bursting in.
Were I a prince indeed and offspring true
Of my dear warrior father, rest his soul,
Would I not strike my uncle's murd'rous head
Clean from's shoulders? Here's the Danish throne,
Upon whose cushions rich have sat eight kings,
Each nobler than the last, until this snake
Whose guile insinuates his slithering words
Into the minds of all he meets, save me,
Annexing power o'er them.

(Addressing the empty throne)

Father dear,
Old Hamlet, rightful King, thy manly blood
Flows in th'unworthy veins of this thy son,
Inflaming me to action. Grant me this!
That I may soon adorn this yearning brow
With Denmark's royal crown, and I shall vow
To rule with justice, wisdom and the good
Of all thy suff'ring citizens in my heart.

VOICE OFF (OLD HAMLET). Swear!

HAMLET. I do swear – upon my very sword!

(Enter Old Hamlet, wearing crown)

OLD HAMLET. Swear!

HAMLET. Upon my life! Upon my … Father?

OLD HAMLET. Aye!
No ghost, but vital substance animate,
As evidenced by this o'erdue embrace.
And as, e'en now, revealed to all the court.
Come in, come in!

(Enter Gertrude, Polonius, Ophelia and Priest)

And let me vouchsafe more
Of the strange circumstance that led to this
Event momentous, which I see hath wrought
New miracle – my son bereft of speech
Which in more normal times does freely flow
Trippingly on's tongue.

HAMLET. I am made dumb.

OLD HAMLET. Aye, fetch us Claudius too!
(Enter Claudius, shackled)

Those bonds severe
Shall clamp their iron fondle 'bout his wrists
'Til he's enwrapped by justice for his crimes.
Know all, then, that my convalescenment
These many moons did keep me from my siege
While yon wise priest did turn about my heart

From flaming vengeful hate to feelings cool
Of calm and comely reconcilement
T'wards Claudius, whose overvaulting pride
And thwarted longings for our nation's crown
Did spur him on to murder. Murder, yea
Most fell. Lo, witness that his villainy failed!
For as I know you know, the friar's draught
Innocuous in its ultimate effect
Did shield my blood from mortal atrophy.

HAMLET. And when in steel all clad we did behold
Thy ghost upon the wintry battlements?

OLD HAMLET. Twas I myself, be-sprited in the mist.

GERTRUDE. And when in ceremonial grief we laid
Thy corpse to stony burial in the earth?

PRIEST. I, with a loyal sexton's burly aid
His Highness to a secret hall did bring,
Where, 'til the bloom of life to him returned
He dwelt up to the present joyful day.

OLD HAMLET. Joyful indeed! For here we take the place
Which by divine decree is rightly ours,
While close beside me, bound by mutual troths,
Made stronger through forgiveness, hers and mine,
For wrongs whatever, done to her or me,
My wife, my Gertrude, glorifies her throne.
And as for Claudius ...

POLONIUS. My Liege, the Law!
For by my office as minister of state,
Although in admiration, nay in awe
At this thy saintly pardon of her faults,
Yet must I set in motion, though it bring
E-motion grievous streaming in its wake;
Or should I say, a-wake e-motion sad,
For thus our gamesome words do double o'er
Their meanings. Let that be. I say the law
Insists no man shall take two wives on pain
Of death by hanging. No, nor woman neither!
The Queen, the Queen must die for she has wed
Two husbands here, and ta'en them both to bed.
I crave your highness' pardon. Speaking plain
Is oftentimes your loyal Polonius' bane.

OLD HAMLET. Did ever sunshine smile upon the Earth
Without some leaden cloud did heave in view
To spoil the beauteous day? Polonius here
Speaks true. Alack the times! My fair belov'd,
Thou art beholden to the nation's laws.
In innocence, believing me deceased,
Thou took my brother's ring. When kings and queens
O'erride the statute, ah, then chaos comes,
The dogs of war do tear apart the peace
And moral order of the sovereign state.
Thou must this stricture harsh obey.

HAMLET. Father and King, thy son kneels down to thee
In supplication for my dam and Queen.

Thy word was innocence, pardon was the theme
Of thy most dear restorement to the throne.
So let again forgiveness flow from thee
To spare this all-unwitting criminal.

OLD HAMLET. The law, I iterate it, must prevail!
Claudius, for treason 'gainst my person dost thou stand
Guilty, and forfeit therefore be thy life.
And likewise, sweetest Gertrude, must thou die,
Though bitter tears do drown my grieving eye.

PRIEST. Hold hard, just king, th'upholder of the right
Of law, and rightly so. The Queen shall live!

POLONIUS. Tush, priest! Be thou advised …

PRIEST. Yet hear me out!

OLD HAMLET. We still have known thee for a holy man,
But plead ye not for us to bend the law!

PRIEST. No flexibility's needed. Good my lord,
Thinkst thou that, cognizant thou wert alive,
I would deliver up the virtuous Queen
Unto a bigamous match? My Sovereign, no!

CLAUDIUS. Deceitful cleric! Twas thy slippery self
Conducted here the ceremony grand
Which did unite the factions of our land.

GERTRUDE. Else had it fallen into civil strife

Had I not, politic, made Claudius' wife.

PRIEST. Such were the self-same reasons I did act
To save our Denmark. Yet, in Heaven's sight
I wed thee not.

GERTRUDE. Alas the day, thou didst!

CLAUDIUS. Thou strumpet friar, serving the shifty times,
To feather still thy nest obsequious,
Preaching but texts thou knowst the powerful
Will pay to hear! Thou spliced us, thoroughly.

PRIEST. Nay! For the rituals I did employ
Were empty repetitions of trite phrase
And echoes only of the sacred writ.
Thou art, my Queen, no more to Claudius bound
In holy matrimony than am I,
Which were indeed a wondrous merry match!

OLD HAMLET. Is this the truth?

PRIEST. It is, my lord.

OLD HAMLET. Then swear!

PRIEST. I swear, and may that curse which rode my back
In Italy once more return to pluck
My fearful soul to Hell, if't be not so.

OLD HAMLET. We are content. It seems, fair Gertrude, now,
That on us once again the blue skies smile.

HAMLET. Father, 'tis so. And with thy kingly leave
I shall have share of this most happy wreck.
Ophelia, I turn and kneel to thee.
Though not of royal lineage direct,
Thy family hath an honourable root,
I have no doubt, when delv'd to origin.
E'en though, fair maid, were thou the daughter mere
Of the most humble swineherd in his cott
I'd ask thee this. To place thy hand in mine
And be my bride.

POLONIUS *(Aside).* More gins t'ensnare the bird
Of innocent youth. Ophelia! Heed my words …

OPHELIA. Father, enough! Prince Hamlet, to my thanks
For tendering such high honour in this wise,
I must I fear append that I decline.
Moreover must I now confess in shame
More falsehood I committed. All those times
I did receive thy overtures of love;
Letters and keepsakes of most touching kind;
I did but lead thee on. Part as decoy
And part as spur, to prick the jealousy
Of him I love.

HAMLET. Who's he?

POLONIUS. Aye, tell us who
And I shall see …

OPHELIA. Father, hold thy tongue!
Your Majesty, I bow beneath your feet
In abject importunement of thy grace.
To celebrate deliverance this day –
For each of us new life, when hope had fled –
I beg thee, grant thy subject here one boon.
And it must follow as the day the night,
Forever shall a canker in this court
Be purged quite out of thy sight and life.

OLD HAMLET. That love we bear thee and thy father sage,
Which Gertrude too in measure full doth share,
Warrants fulfilment of thy plea. So speak!
Define this boon which, granted here to thee
Shall bless the giver also, in such wise?

OPHELIA. My lord, thou knowest me.

OLD HAMLET. As maiden pure!

OPHELIA. Then must this signify the hour when all
My sins remembered be. I have a love.
This I confessed already. I do beg,
Your Majesty, that now, this very eve
He banish'd be for ever from the realm,
Where nevermore shall I behold his face.

OLD HAMLET. Strange love, and stranger plea! But state his name
And he upon the instant takes his leave,
Escorted to the border of our land,
And not return, on pain of certain death.
His name is?

OPHELIA. Claudius.

OLD HAMLET. Speak clearer, child!

OPHELIA. Claudius! Claudius!

OLD HAMLET. My brother?

OPHELIA. He.

(Gertrude rises, swoons)

OLD HAMLET. Polonius, see you to the stricken Queen!

POLONIUS. I shall. Your Highness, take my arm. This way.
Who did she say?
OPHELIA. My Claudius! My lord!

(Exeunt Gertrude and Polonius)

OLD HAMLET. My brother? He who in foul treason steep'd
Did seek to steal our life, our wife, our crown?

Plotted to slay our son, and turned our court
Into a wassail house of swaggering sots?
You love him and would have me spare his life?

HAMLET. Ophelia! That? Why? Why this curlike fiend?

OPHELIA. He is a man, take him for all in all,
The first and last that I shall ever serve.
They say best men are moulded out of faults,
And from this dictum do I take my cue.
His banishment shall save his precious life,
Which otherwise were forfeit to the law.
And he and I in exile labour shall
To expurgate the guilt we've here accrued.

OLD HAMLET. Nay! To a nunnery get, for Claudius dies.
This is my regal will, and granite set.

PRIEST. My lord, a word!

OLD HAMLET. Nay, priest, I am resolv'd.
Too long have I delayed in fruitless reason.
Take him to execution for his treason!
There is some limit to my stock of pardons.

PRIEST. The quantity of Mercy is not weighed!
Nor is it pertinent to Claudius' fate.
King Hamlet, thou didst grant Ophelia's boon,
And as a King who'd see proud Denmark dwell
In honesty and truth and rule of law,

Thou must stand steadfast now to honour thy word
And be a King in deed as much as name.

OLD HAMLET. Thou good old priest! Once more thy counsels sound
Do guide my steps from rage to wisdom. So!
Usurper rank, it seems thou art escap'd
From peril imminent of judicial death.
And with this maid, whose love thou not deserves,
Take thou thy leave of Denmark! Loose his chains!

CLAUDIUS. Oh, my offence was foul. It stinks to the skies.
But now. Now not possess'd of those effects
For which I sought to rob thee of thy breath,
Good brother, I may sue for pardon sweet
Of heaven, and atone for myriad crimes
With life of virtue, charity and love
In consort with my fair Ophelia.

OPHELIA. King Hamlet, may God's benison remain
O'er thee and all the blessed land of Dane!

(Exeunt Ophelia and Claudius)

HAMLET. Adieu, adieu! Remember me!

(Enter Gertrude)

GERTRUDE. I am recovered.

OLD HAMLET. Welcome, chuck!

(They kiss)

GERTRUDE. Wait, friar!
Why creeps thou thus so stealthily away?

OLD HAMLET. Good holy man, hold hard! This long day's work
With reconcilement, evil deeds put right
And common good to all, is foremost thine.
Yet mystery surrounds thee. What's thy name?

PRIEST. Lawrence, my lord.

GERTRUDE. Whence came you?

PRIEST. From the plains
Of Italy, where dwelt I 'til the time
When gloomy peace o'erhung the city fair
Which harboured me.

HAMLET. Why gloom? Was sorrow there?

PRIEST. Aye, by this hand! For dismal fate decreed
A pair of star-cross'd lovers met their end
That would not, had I prudent silence kept,
And not have interfered. But now at last
In Elsinore perhaps I have restor'd
Fresh life in lieu of what was then cut short.

HAMLET. Reviving, Friar Lawrence, all who here
Were dead to th'world, with one exception!
(Picking up skull and addressing it)

For all are newly leased with life but thee!

PRIEST. Who?

HAMLET. Poor Yorick, alas! Father's old jester! See!

PRIEST. Ah. Nay.

GERTRUDE. Not Yorick's skull. It could not be.

HAMLET. Why, three and twenty years since, lay this bone!
(Embarrassed silence)
The sexton so reported.

GERTRUDE. He was wrong.
That jester quit our land in deepest shame.
In banishment!

HAMLET. For what? What heinous crime?

PRIEST. For love, that dared to risk what lovers do
Despite the pride of kingship.

OLD HAMLET. Woah, old priest!
Thou knowst not of such matters. Hamlet, list!
Come close, for what I'll now to thee impart
Touches thee close, my dearest only son.
(*Intimately – a family huddle*)
Ere my beloved Gertrude was my bride
Already was she bless'd, though small, with child.
And I, enamoured with my beauteous Queen,

Presumed him mine. But when five year had pass'd ...

GERTRUDE. I was in total love with my mate's soul!

OLD HAMLET. ... she did confess the lapse, rather than nurse
A single secret 'tween us. She I shrove
But into exile the natural father sent.

HAMLET. Hath borne me on his back a thousand times,
This Yorick! Soft! My slow wit's stream has but
This moment oozed to meet the sea of truth.
Yorick? My father?
(A pause. Taking it in)
What became of him?

GERTRUDE. In Italy, fam'd for its music, dance,
Its sculpture, architecture, all the arts;
And for the gracious living of its lords;
Exists a class of lumpen peasants too,
Whose life doth scarce surpass the mindless beast.
Such plebs do oftentimes their animals
Keep in at doors. As banished Yorick once
Did stroll about the city in the sun,
Lo! From a high-flung tenement there fell
A pig, a monster of a sow. Scarce ere
The shadow of this fatal hog loomed dark
About his person, Yorick's soul had flew,
Crushed from his body by the creature's bulk.
In life our merry jester filled the court
With laughter and with music through the day.

So, by his droll and unexpected end
He brings smiles still to all who hear of it.

OLD HAMLET. Thy father was a king of jesters once.
Therefore the blood within thy veins is royal.
And now this King of Denmark is thy da
And loves thee more than ever father could
That Nature gave thee. Come into my arms!

(They embrace. Exit Priest)

HAMLET. How learnt you of old Yorick's strange demise?

GERTRUDE. By letter from a cleric of that place.
A monk who wrote he knew poor Yorick well.

HAMLET. And in which town was this?

GERTRUDE. Verona! Why?

OLD HAMLET. Friar! Knew you that city? Why, he's gone!

(Enter Polonius)

POLONIUS. My lord, I have news for you.
Th'ambassadors
From England are arrived and with this word.
That Rosencrantz and Guildenstern are

(Blackout)

Thus Osric ended his drama, with the mysterious word 'blackout'. By then, as any reader will have gathered, I had left the stage, resolved to hasten to my retirement in the abbey at Roskilde. I had come too close for comfort to revealing my past identity and thus the transgression of my banishment. No longer could I stay at Elsinore.

Here I shall spend whatever days the Lord allows me. My confessions I shall pass to the old Abbot and then consign them to a secret hiding place within the abbey's ancient masonry. I am free to do this knowing that my dear son can now look forward to inheriting the throne of Denmark. The rest is silence. Blackout.

Appendix

Translator's Footnote

There has been much favourable response to Osric's play. However, several notable theatre practioners have commented that the play is too short to comprise an evening's entertainment; and yet too long to be seen as a one-act play suitable for festivals.

As a consequence of this, I have presumed to take upon myself to create a 'Curtain-Raiser'; in effect a related piece to augment 'Hamlet Act Six'. Taken together, the two could provide a complete evening's performance.

My contribution is entitled 'Hamlet Act Postmodern'. As Mr Terry Eagleton has written in The Guardian: "Postmodernism is meant to be fun, even if a current of nihilism runs steadily beneath it". I hope that an audience might find it so. The cast is similar in numbers to that of Osric's masterpiece and may therefore employ the same players.

Hamlet Act Postmodern

By Dennis Harkness

The characters
H: Hamlet
A: Artistic Director
M: Mrs Mopp (aka props mistress)
L: Lighting and Sound Technician
E: Elected Representative
T: Top Person
X,Y, &Z = 3 US Scientists = L,E, &T (above)

The action takes place

(An empty stage. Above, a screen for either Surtitles or, better, projected words and pictures. As the audience enters, they see a series of slides, numbered as occurs in the script. On most

of these are words initialled P M. These two letters should be highlighted. More are shown as the action continues).

1] **PostModern**
2] Pic of a **Pomo** building
3] **PoMo**
4] **Pic** – eg Tracy Emin's bed
5] **Post Modern**
6] **Pic** – eg Ian McKellan as Hamlet?

(As house lights fade,, the stage fills rapidly with very obvious hissing mist, to suggest the battlements at Elsinore).

7] **Posterior Movement** – wriggling of bums on seats

(Enter H, dressed as a conventional Hamlet; moves to centre stage and adopts an angst-ridden pose).

8] **PreaMble – please be patient**

H
To be …
(This is as far as she gets. Enter A, as the Director, in modern dress. She is tense.)

A
Hold it, hold it right there!

H
Wha? …
(A glances nervously at the back row of the audience; whispers in H's ear; indicates that a certain person is sat there.)

A
'Tser

(A indicates H should exit. H nods in agreement; exits squinting into the darkened house and trips slightly as she goes. A makes sure she's gone, then turns to the audience. Opens her mouth to speak when M enters.)

9] **Props Mistress**

(She's older, in apron, hair rollers and slippers; with a fag hanging from her mouth. She's carrying a lectern and a duster. Plonks down the lectern, perfunctorily wipes it, peers at the audience, sniffs, blows her nose into the duster and shambles off.)

A
Thank you
(A takes up her position behind the lectern. Before she can speak, M returns with a folding director's chair. She unfolds the chair and flops down to face the lectern. Looking round, she realises she's spoiling someone's sightline, gets up with a tut and a grunt, and moves. A waits for her to settle. M kicks off a slipper, heaves a huge sigh of relief; then flips off the other, which flies into the audience. She gestures for someone to throw or to bring it back. Insists, if necessary. She makes herself comfortable. A looks at her for permission to speak. M nods, but immediately bursts into a prolonged fit of smoker's coughing. A stage manager (or a plant in the audience), gives her a throat sweet. A watches all this in resignation. At last, she is about to speak when from the wings bustles L, with a clip-on mic.)

L
We can't hear you, love
(L starts pulling A's clothing about)

L
Try this

10] **Personal Mic**

(L fusses about with the mic and a lead which has to go under A's topclothes and down her back; plus a battery pack which, having no pockets, A ends up holding in her hand.)

L
There you go, sweetheart!
(A looks daggers but L is oblivious. She's cool and gives the audience a big smile and a wave as she exits. A clears her throat. The first few words are characterised by alternating high and low volumes as if someone offstage is struggling to get the levels right.)

A
Good morning, ladies and gentlemen! Or should I say good afternoon? Or Good even, even; even 'evening all'! Seeing as it is PM. Post Mid-day. Yes, I can remember when there WAS a mid-day post! *(she giggles).*

11] **Post Meridian**

Perhaps I ought to say 'post-meridian' … as in Emma, the Jane Austen, … erm … Emma Thompson, the Jane Austen playwright?
But that's quite enough pandering to the luvvies *(she giggles again)*. Perhaps I should enjoy myself. Introduce you. I'm A. I'm the Artistic Director of our little production of 'Hamlet Act Six'.

I … AH … (she bursts into song, finger flicking fingers to the rhythm) AAAH was born one mornin' when the sun didn' shine;

12] **Popular Music – of the 50s** (please don't clap)

Ah picked up mah shovel an' ah walked to the mine.
Ah loaded sixteen tons of number nine coal.
(she breaks off, as a thought strikes her)
Number nine coal? I wonder now, would that be anthracite? Or bituminous – that's a lot more tarry, as you might guess from the name. It might even be steam coal … that
(Here her voice gradually fades. She absent-mindedly strokes herself)

13] **Priapic Moment**

Would be more, more … steamy. SSSteamy.
(She takes a deep breath, and wakes up)
Anyway. Enough about me! Welcome, everybody, boys and girls, men and women, and men, to today's performance. I do hope, most sincerely, and I mean that, folks, you're going to enjoy it. Just one announcement – if any of you here present know of any just cause or impediment …
(E, another woman, power dressed, strides down the aisle onto the stage.)

E
Yes! I do!

14] **Personal Magnetism**

(A yields her the lectern, deferentially)

E

As I'm sure you are aware, I'm Peter Mandelson, your former member of parliament for Hartlepool. Hartlepool. *(relishing the word)*, Haaart – le-pool. Heart *(clasping her fist to her breast)* Le Poul! *(Cheekily flicking her hips and pursing her lips)* But you can call me PM! Oops, I forgot. Silly me! *(slapping her wrist)*. Because, Your Royal Majesties, My Lords, Ladies and Gentlemen it is my deep and profoundest pleasure to invite on stage the real PM. Yes, she's here tonight in this very theyater, the Pee-rime Minister of England and Wales and Scotsland and Northern and Ireland, not forgetting good old Heart-le-pewle, to step up here and cut the blah blah blah, I mean the ribbon.

15] **Prime Miniskirt**

(A and M make their way to the back of the audience to a crescendo of fanfare, collect T, a blue-rinse woman in a suit, and escort her to the stage. She takes her place behind the lectern. As the cast-led applause subsides, she speaks)

T

War, war, war, whart happens in Hamlet? That is the question. But war, war, war, is that the answer? No, my friends. The answer, my friends (she sings) is blowin' in the wind.

16] **Popular Music – of the Sixties**

The answer is (they all join in, harmonising the last long note) blowin' in the wind.
(They all pose, for applause. The over-loud hiss of stage fog resumes. Exeunt L,E and T. The others watch as H enters, balletically, Carrying before her a skull, complete with jaw. She stops, delicately feels inside one eye-socket and draws out a long string of gaudy silk handkerchiefs.)

17] **Prestidigitary Moment**

Which she throws to M. From the other eyehole she brings a white cloth folded into a ball. She places the skull on the lectern, facing the audience. She unfolds the cloth.From it she picks up and holds high between forefinger and thumb a tiny crystal. A sharp spotlight picks it out)

18] **Pm – atomic number 61**

H (whispering)
I offer you … Promethium
(Enter, running, X,Y and Z, American scientists in white coats (and bald wigs?))

X
Hi, everybody! I'm Marinsky!

Y
And I'm Glendenin! Hi there!

Z

And you know who I am … Any guesses? C'mon, no need to be bashful. Pardon me? Yeah, of course you knew. I am the one and only C.D.Coryell. And you know what?

X
We

Y
Discovered

Z
Promethium!!
(A triumphal pose. M sniffs. A reprise)

X
We

Y
Discovered

Z
PROMETHIUM!!!

M
I always use sennapods meself. Promethywot?

X
Promethium! YOU know . Chemical symbol Pm!

Y
It's a rare earth. A RARE earth! O, rare earth, that hath such wonders in it.

Z
The very last to be discovered!

X
In nineteen forty seven!

Y

Boiling point two thousand and sixty degrees. Celsius!

Z

And just you guess where we found it

H

PM? In a skull?

X

Nope, I am not Pia Mater.

A

In a mortuary?

Y

Eh?

A

Are you found in a morgue?

Y

No, I am not a post Mortem

M

Was it in Oak Ridge, Tennessee?

Z

Aw, who told ya?

X

Never mind THAT

19] **Psychotic Moodswing**

What do YOU know, about Oak Ridge?

Y
Cool it, Marinsky!

X
You some kinda Commie Dyke, uh? UH??

20] **Pincer Movement**

(X is restrained by Y and Z)

Z
Marinsky! Enough already. So the dame knows sommat she shouldn't oughta, so we play it cool, OK? Lady! My friend here is kinda curious. Can you tell us whatcher know about Oak Ridge.? About the … Manhattan Project?

21] **Project Manhattan**

M
Nuffink

X
Oh yeah? How come you've heard of it in the first place?
(M shuffles across to X, who takes a nervous step backwards. She taps him on the chest)

M
There!
(X stares down at his breast pocket, on which is inscribed 'Oak Ridge Tennessee'. The three scientist grin. As they turn, we see their backs and the written 'Oak Ridge – the best noocleer bomb lab in the world. Their part is played. They shake hands with the other actors and members of the audience.)

A
Hang on a mo, Geronimo. Why did you name it Prom, ... Prom.

Y *(from the auditorium)*
Promethium? After Prometheus. Remember, he stole fire from the gods and gave it to mankind.

A
And can you tell us what this stuff is used for?

Z
Negative! You want facts, you're in the wrong play
(Exeunt X, Y & Z)

A *(calls after them)*
But I love facts.
(She lines up behind the lectern. In lecture mode)
For example, The Prominent Moth. The Prominent Moth is so called because of the prominent protuberances on its wings and thorax.

22] **Prominent Moth – family Notodontidae**

It possesses ... it possesses ... a stout, hairy body
(She starts fantasising again, stroking her cheek and neck, as her voice weakens)
The larva, when disturbed, can raise both ends of its body. It vibrates its prolegs and (she gulps) squirts a fluid, to a distance of several inches. Bright colouration warns predators of its bad taste. Pupation ... pupation takes place ... underground.
This ani ... mal ... belongs to the family ... Not ... o ... don't ... I ... dieeee.

23] **Priapic Moment Number 2**

(She stands there in rapt silence)

M
Mmmmm! You DO like facts, don't you!

H
Look here, this is no help to me at all. The dynamic of flexibility required to deliver an on-going manifesto of dramatic constructivism just isn't there.

M
Eh? I think I'll go and make a cup of tea.
(She exits, sniffing)

H
Are you listening?
(A stops day dreaming)

A
Of course I am

H
What do you think, then?

A
I think … what was it you said?

H
Oh, forget it! Can we get back to the play? You're the Director. So, tell me, how are we going to do the gravedigger scene in postmodern mode,

24] **Pretentious Mumbo-jumbo**

While delivering a proto-marxist agenda which avoids the non-binary pitfalls of an excessively

simplistic alienatory stylisation and yet shrugs off the claustrophobic mantle inherited from Peter Brook?
(A considers this)

A
Eureka!

H
Well?

A
We'll cut it.

H
CUT IT??
(A nods, decisively)

H
The whole gravedigger scene? Even 'Alas, poor Yorick'?

A
Er, … Yep! We'll deconstruct Yorick, the diggers, the lot. We'll go straight on to the funeral.
(Immediately, M,L,E and T enter bearing a coffin, which they lower to the ground, or, better, into a trap, if there is one)

L *(as Laertes)*
Must there no more be done?

25] **Patched together Masterwork**

M *(as extremely stern priest)*
No more be done:
We should profane the service of the dead
To sing a requiem, and such rest to her
As to peace-departed souls.

L *(in priest's face)*
I tell thee, churlish priest,
A ministering angel shall my sister be
When thou liest howling.

H
What? The fair Ophelia? This is I,
Hamlet the Dane!

L
The devil take thy soul!

26] **Pugilistic Moment**

(They grapple and wrestle. The other four stand, as the corners of a boxing ring. A bell sounds for the end of the round. H and L retire to their corners, using T and M's knees as stools. E turns to the audience. During the following, A,L,M and T carry the coffin away)

E
So there you have it. Shakespeare, the first post-modernist, the primary pomo, the bard of Hart-le-pool; or icon of the age of cybergenetics? Take your pick, the choice is yours, ladies and gentlemen. And, to help you decide …
(L sets up a flip chart on an easel. T returns with a pointer)
What we have here is … anybody? … Correct, a 'flip' chart.

27] **Patronising Manner**

And if we 'flip' a page over (E does so), we find a 'mind-map' of the play itself. Here at its heart is H for

Hamlet and, radiating from the man himself – and what a piece of work is HE – are the factors in his dilemma. His Uncle Claudius, his mother, his would-be girl-friend; his history of being performed by all the big names for four hundred years; his name exploited to promote cheap cigars; and so on and so forth, which I believe is a quote from Anna and the King of Siam – further evidence of just how overburdened is this play, with cultural badges.

(Enter A. E takes away the flip chart, goes off chatting to T)

A

Thank you, professor! And now, on with the action, the motley, the show – must go on. But before curtain up, is there anybody here from … Denmark? No? Oh, pity, I had a really funny joke about Hans Christian Anderson and the Little Mermaid. (she giggles) Oh, well, never mind!

(A steps aside. Enter H as Hamlet and L as Horatio. They sweep across the stage , deep in conversation. All we hear is —)

H

… things in heaven and earth, Horatio, than are dreamed of in your philos …

(Exeunt H and L. A comes forward)

A

Philosophy! Aha! The clue to our prince's problem – it lies in semiology. If we seek to decode his behaviour, we must also dismember his view of a complex world; of the court at Elsinore, of his mother's o'erhasty marriage to her late husband's brother, etcetera, etcetera. But, as the old song goes, *(she sings)*

28] **Popular Music – of the Seventies**

Nobody does it better. And nobody COULD do it better – than Will Shakespeare!

(Enter M, as WS in full bard's outfit, quill pen, bald pate, the lot. Goes to the lectern, while E enters as TV type quizmaster, accompanied by L, as glamorous assistant.)

E

Let's play DECONSTRUCT!!!

(piped applause and wild cheers & shrieks)

Would our first contestant please introduce herself/himself?

M *(as WS, with a Brummie accent?)*

Well, Peter, my name is Bill. I'm a Bard, and I'm from STRATFORD UPON AVON!

(More piped applause)

29] **Playfulness Merely**

E

Bill has chosen as his special subject The Life and Crimes of Claudius the King, but I don't need to tell you that in DECONSTRUCT, we don't care what the contestant says. It's the audience that counts, and let me take this opportunity to say to all you good folks at home, that here tonight we have a studio audience that is just FAN-TASTIC!

(More piped applause)

Bill, I have to tell you that our wonderful audience here has voted for a different specialist subject for you, and that is

(L prances accross and hands E a large golden envelope. From it, E extracts a large golden card, and reads out …)
What Happens in Hamlet!
(More piped applause)
So, Bill, are you ready to play DECONSTRUCT?

M
Yes, Peter.

E
Your first question, then, for ten groats, and you won't get too many of those to the Euro, is this, and please listen carefully. Which came first, was it … A) the chicken, or … B) the egg, or … C) the omelette, or … D) Rosencrantz? Time's up, oh what a shame, you go away with … nothing. But I can tell you that if you'd said A you would have been richer by seventy-five drachma, as the correct order is A then B then C, followed by D. Every fool can tell that. Just because you wrote the collected works of George W Shakeshaft, you seem to think you can come here to the Twenty-first Century and teach us all there is to know about human nature. Well, too bad, Mr Cleverclogs from Stratford Upon Avon.
(M stands impassive at the lectern, then picks up the skull, examines it pensively. Takes it upstage. The audience sees that across her back is a macdonalds ad. Exeunt E and L. The lights fade, except for a spot picking out H who comes downstage carrying the skull in one hand. With the other she operates the jaw to mime the words it addresses to the audience:)

30] **Puppetry Moment**

H
If our passing pageant here
Hath warmed the heart and pleased the ear;
If we've touched the minds of men,
Then our toils Olympian
Have proved their worth, and given cause
For you to bless us, with … applause!
(One after another, A,M,L,E and T run on to take a bow. They remain in a line, smiling and bowing until well after the clapping completely subsides. H has placed the skull upstage. The lights stay up. The actors look at each other doubtfully. Then:)

A *(to the others)*
Well, what do you think?

E
Hmmm …

A
Go ahead, be honest. They *(indicating the audience)* can take it. Half of them are on comps anyway.

31] **Post curtain-call Misgiving**

E
Well, I don't think the house was much cop at all. I mean, some of them failed to get even a tenth of the contemporary allusions. I mean, like, some of the older ones over there, I'd hazard a guess that they've no idea what Post Modernism IS.

L
Yeah, right, like you DO, uh?

E

Meaning?

(L has turned her back on E and is whispering to M and sniggering)

MEANING?

L

Meaning that your poncey script is a load of deconstructed SHIT!

(There is a silence)

A

Erm … We've got a fortnight of this show to run. I don't think that kind of language is conducive to a happy ship.

E

You SAID it. But you said it too late. I'm leaving. (to T) You coming, sugarplum?

(T smiles sheepishly at the others, then exits, hand in hand with E)

L

How uncool is that!

(A further silence. L smiles at the audience and shrugs)

L

I'll do the lights.

(She goes into the wings. The lights fade and working lights come on. M is slightly apart. H and A stare helplessly at each other.)

H

What about Hamlet Act Six?

A
That's a completely different kettle of more matter with less art. I need a drink. Come on.

(Exeunt A and H. This leaves M, still dressed as Shakespeare. A brightening spotlight picks her out. She opens her mouth to deliver an unforgettable punchline, then her head drops. She examines the quill. In despair she shuffles back to the lectern and carries it off. Upstage, the skull remains, spotlit, grinning at the audience.)

CURTAIN

Acknowledgements

My thanks to the numerous ones without whom this book wouldn't exist. To W.S., for his incomparable plays (my humble offerings come with deepest respect). To the other members of the Bridgwater University of the Third Age Creative Writing Group Two, for encouraging me to scribble on.

To Alison Paine, who directed the first staging of Hamlet Act Six, with Shakespeare Live (and to Gill Morrell, head of that theatre company).

Above all, to Terence Sackett, for transforming my typescript into a book; and to Juliet, my patient, talented and industrious beloved Better Half.

Printed in Poland
by Amazon Fulfillment
Poland Sp. z o.o., Wrocław